MY IRANIAN
REVOLUTION

MY IRANIAN REVOLUTION

John Robert Tipton

iUniverse LLC
Bloomington

My Iranian Revolution

iUniverse books may be ordered through booksellers or by contacting:

iUniverse LLC
1663 Liberty Drive
Bloomington, IN 47403
www.iuniverse.com
1-800-Authors (1-800-288-4677)

ISBN: 978-1-4917-0689-3 (sc)
ISBN: 978-1-4917-0691-6 (hc)
ISBN: 978-1-4917-0690-9 (e)

Printed in the United States of America

iUniverse rev. date: 10/05/2013

CHAPTER I

The overseas telephone service had been down for more than a week due to a strike by the telephone workers union in support of the revolution. Our last contact with Fort Worth was through the weekly pouch that was delivered every Wednesday afternoon. But now even the pouch service abruptly ceased, as civilian and commercial aircraft were forbidden to fly in Iranian airspace. Only the military was authorized to be airborne to prevent Ayatollah Khomeini's return from Paris. Our communication with the outside world had been severed, and it was now impossible to evacuate from Iran. The end was nigh.

I sometimes wondered how I got myself into this mess. I now know I should be more careful what I ask for. It seems long ago and far away, but I still recall it all quite well as though it was yesterday.

On the Dallas side of my commute, traffic was heavier than usual, and I soon encountered a sea of red taillights. It was a Monday morning, and I was on my way to work from my home in East Dallas to the Shell Helicopter Company located on the eastern side of Fort Worth. I'd been dealing with this sixty-mile round-trip for the past two years.

I had graduated from the University of Texas in Austin with a bachelor of science in accounting. After working for three years with a small accounting firm in Dallas, I was hired on as a supervisor in accounts payable with Shell Helicopter and supervised six union-covered employees.

I made it to work on time that morning, but as I pulled into the company parking lot, it occurred to me that I was no longer as happy with things as I used to be. My commute was oppressive, and I was tired of dealing with my unionized employees. But most importantly, my beautiful wife had recently left me and filed for a divorce. I knew my life needed a change, but I didn't have a clue concerning the direction of my new path.

It was the summer of 1977, and the Shell Helicopter Company announced receiving a significant contract from the government of Iran. This contract couldn't have come along at a better time, as Shell's military business had plummeted two years earlier with the end of the Vietnam War in 1975. The company had relied primarily on its commercial helicopter business since that time.

The contract Shell Helicopter received from Iran included the design and construction of a state-of-the-art helicopter-manufacturing facility near Isfahan. This ancient city, known for its beautiful Islamic architecture, is located in the central part of Iran, south of Tehran.

Upon completion of this facility, Shell, along with its Iranian counterparts, would begin manufacturing several different helicopter models that were already in production in Fort Worth. The ultimate goal was to eventually turn over a self-functioning helicopter industry to the Iranian government. The US government had sanctioned this contract and gave Shell its authorization and approval to proceed.

As I walked to my office building, it occurred to me that the new Iranian contract perhaps offered the perfect opportunity for me to leave my old life behind and start anew. I knew then I had to somehow throw my hat into the ring with the adventurous goal of eventually relocating to Iran and building helicopters.

My manager was Ray Cole, a middle-aged, bespectacled, balding man whom I respected and thought of as the friendly guy next door. We got along quite well, and I always performed my best for Ray. He would then reward me once a year with a decent performance evaluation and pay raise.

I noticed Ray's office door was open this morning, and I could see he was alone. I knew it would be a good opportunity to talk about the Iranian contract, so I knocked on his door, stuck my head inside the doorway, and smiled. "Hey, Ray, good morning! Got a minute?" I asked.

He replied, "Good morning, John. Sure, come on in and have a seat. What's on your mind?"

I then entered his office and sat down in the upholstered armchair opposite his desk. "I know that this sounds a little crazy, but I've decided my life needs a change," I said. "I would be interested in transferring to Iran with the new contract. I realize it's premature at this time, but do you think there will be any accounting jobs opening up over there that would interest me?"

He seemed a bit surprised and then looked up at me over the top of his reading glasses as he replied, "You're not premature at all. We were briefed just last Friday by the contracts manager on a recent change to the Iranian contract. This change will result in an immediate opening in Tehran that I think will definitely interest you."

Ray then explained that Shell was now contractually obligated to provide six manager-level positions to interface with our customer, Sauzi Helicopter Iran (Iranian Helicopter Industry), in its headquarters building in downtown Tehran. The six managerial positions would represent the Shell Helicopter departments of finance, engineering, facilities, training, procurement, and logistics. Each manager would coordinate with and assist the appropriate Iranian air force general who handled that particular department. The Shell finance manager would be responsible to interface with and assist the air force general in charge of matters of finance.

Ray continued. "We do have a scheduling problem, as the Iranian air force wants this all to have happened yesterday. Our vice president has identified these open positions as top priority items for his weekly status meeting, which I attend. Because none of Shell's managers, including me, are interested in moving out of their comfort zone and laterally transferring to Tehran, we've either got to hire from the outside or promote from within. If we follow our procedures to process this requisition through the personnel department, advertise these positions, and go through the interview cycle, this could take forever. But if we promote from within, our hands are no longer tied by these constraints. I would hate to lose you, but if you're seriously interested, you are my only qualified candidate, and I'm willing to recommend you for the job."

I just couldn't believe my ears as I thought to myself, *Wow! I just walked into the office this morning and casually asked Ray about some future unknown job in Iran. Now, a half hour later, he is going to recommend me for the manager of finance position in the new Tehran headquarters. How lucky can a guy be? Talk about being in the right place at just the right time!*

"I am definitely interested," I said. *Here I am,* I thought, *a twenty-seven-year-old, free-spirited young man from a small oil field town in East Texas. I'm now to be promoted to a manager's position by a major aircraft company and moving to the far side of the earth where I'll be dealing with an Iranian general. I'd really never been out of the United States before except for an afternoon spent in a Nuevo Laredo cantina on the banks of the Rio Grande.*

Ray said, "We envision that the finance manager's position in Tehran will essentially have three bosses and will require a little juggling to keep everyone happy. You will answer directly to the Tehran headquarters manager in support of the day-to-day operations, and you will respond to my office on a dotted line in matters of financial policy and procedure. In addition, you will be required to interface as needed with the Iranian air force general responsible for the financial affairs of Sauzi Helicopter Iran. His name is General Ghorbani. His office provides the funding for our contract, so it's very important to Shell's bottom line that you take care of General Ghorbani's every need. You may even have to remind him when the next quarterly contract payment comes due."

Ray then added, "You will have to go through an interview with the newly hired Tehran headquarters manager. His name is Ben Halley, and he is a recently retired air force colonel who previously commanded an entire wing down in San Antonio. He's only going to be here for a few days before heading to Tehran, so I'll arrange your interview—probably sometime this afternoon."

I then returned to my desk and began updating my résumé. Ray called about a half hour later and said my interview had been scheduled with Ben at two o'clock in the nearby conference room just down the hall.

Promptly at two o'clock, I entered the open door of the conference room and could see Ben sitting at the head of the rectangular table. He was perusing through a stack of papers I was certain had relevance to the Iranian contract and my new job.

As I entered the room, I gathered my first impressions of Ben. I could see he was a blue-eyed, square-jawed man in his midfifties with salt-and-pepper hair cut into a medium high-and-tight flattop. As he stood up to introduce himself, I noticed he was about six feet tall and was in decent shape with a few extra pounds

5

around the middle. He was wearing a blue suit that was more of a navy blue than an air force blue—but I still got the subtlety. I also recognized him as being a native Texan when I heard him speak with the familiar Texas twang.

After briefly exchanging some friendly small talk, I handed Ben my newly updated résumé. He then reviewed it and inquired about my background, education, and work experience. His interview sounded so matter-of-fact that I could see he was just going through the motions. It was obvious to me I had the job.

After inquiring about my qualifications, Ben removed a four-by-six color photograph from his stack of documents and explained, "This is a picture of our headquarters building that's located at 107 Sepahbod Zahedi Street in downtown Tehran. It's just a few blocks northwest of the US embassy."

As I briefly studied the picture, I could see it was a newly constructed, five-story, flat-roofed building with aluminum-cased sliding windows on the upper stories. The first floor was clad in polished off-white marble tiles with the upper levels finished with brown masonry.

It looked as though the building had been initially designed with two front entrances intended for two different tenants. Now, there was only one entrance in the middle of the structure. You could clearly see there had originally been another entrance on the right-hand corner.

Now that the entire building would be occupied by only one tenant, the corner entrance had been remodeled and closed up using the same marble tiles. However, the closure plan failed to remove the wide stairway or restore the building's corner. This resulted in a peculiar design of a stairway that led to nowhere on the now-flat corner.

Sauzi Helicopter Iran Building in downtown Tehran

There was a large round medallion on the wall above the double-glassed front doors that opened into the lobby. Along the upper curved outside edge of the medallion were raised letters stating first in the Farsi alphabet, Sauzi Helicopter Iran. It was followed underneath along the bottom edge with The Iranian Helicopter Industry written in English.

In the upper middle of the medallion was a three-dimensional image of a Shell Huey Viper Helicopter. This is a utility-type helicopter that was widely used in Vietnam. It was one of the helicopter models Sauzi Helicopter Iran planned to manufacture upon completion of its new facility near Isfahan.

Ben then further explained, "The Iranian air force generals that run the operation and their civilian staff are already in place on the fourth and fifth floors. We will occupy the second floor and perhaps part of the first floor if needed. Sauzi Helicopter Iran has contracted with Shell to construct a full-service cafeteria with an executive dining room for the generals on the third floor. In

7

addition, we will be building a media room with rear-projection capability and auditorium-type seating in the northwest corner of the first floor. Shell in Fort Worth will provide the engineering, and the Tehran headquarters' staff will handle the contracting and construction management."

Ben continued, "The Iranian air force's schedule is to have this construction completed as soon as possible. Our helicopter facility is still in the design phase, and not one spade of dirt has been turned in Isfahan. But as you can see, we already have a big task ahead of us. I'll be leaving in three days for Tehran, and if you would like to come onboard, it would be great to have you."

I could now feel the firm grip of temptation and knew I couldn't say no as I replied, "Well, thanks, Ben, but before I say yes, I just wanted to ask you about my promotion and the compensation package for in-country employees."

Ben laughed as he said, "Oh yeah, I almost forgot about your promotion and the compensation package."

He then shuffled through his stack of papers again and pulled out a compensation package that outlined the salary and benefits a Shell employee would receive while working in Iran.

He then handed it to me and explained, "First of all, I'm prepared to offer you a 10 percent increase to your base salary for your promotion from supervisor to manager. If this is acceptable, then you'll get a 25 percent increase to your new base salary upon relocation to Iran. In addition, due to your in-country single status, you will be given a monthly housing allowance of eight hundred dollars. Also, your transportation will be provided to and from work. Furthermore, you will earn one week of R&R (rest and relaxation) time for every six months spent in-country and the value of a round-trip coach ticket to your home of record. This will be in addition to your annual vacation you currently enjoy. Also, every six months you will be authorized to receive a thirty-five-pound care package of anything you need shipped from Fort Worth at Shell's expense. Finally, if you meet the physical presence test by residing outside the United States for 330 days out of each year, you will qualify for the Federal Overseas Tax Exemption, and your entire income will be completely tax-free.

"Now, if all of this is acceptable, you will be required to sign a contract agreeing to work in Iran for two years. If you breach this agreement with an early departure, you will be required to reimburse Shell for the cost of relocating you to Iran."

With a big grin on my face, and tempted by the dollar signs now dancing around in my head, I replied, "That sounds great, Ben! I'll have no problem staying in Iran for two years. It'll be a total breeze for me. Just show me where to sign on that dotted line!"

He answered, "That's the responsibility of Shell's personnel department, so they'll have to handle that end of things. I'll give personnel the heads-up on your promotion and transfer. They already understand the urgency of this matter, so they should be getting in touch with you shortly."

"In addition, if you don't have one already, you'll have to apply for an expedited US passport. Shell personnel will then be responsible for sending your passport to the Iranian Consulate in Houston to obtain the multiple exit-reentry visa and residency permit. Both will get stamped inside your passport on the visa pages."

"There are also some immunizations required prior to departure. You will have to be vaccinated for typhoid, and you'll need a DT shot for diphtheria and tetanus. In addition, a gamma globulin injection is recommended to boost your immunity for hepatitis. The Iranian Consulate also requires a negative PPD skin test for tuberculosis prior to issuing a visa. Lastly, while yellow fever is not prevalent in Iran, if you travel outside the United States, it's best you be vaccinated."

Ben then paused in thought before continuing. "There is one more thing you will need. You'll have to get an international driver's license if you intend to drive there. The international driver's license allows you to legally drive in another participating country when accompanied by your valid Texas license. The Iranians will honor this license, and you will not be required to apply for an Iranian driver license."

I could see Ben was clearly in charge, and although his mission had changed, he was still very much a US Air Force wing commander. Most colonels retire, but few ever leave the military. They typically take their military culture, acquired through years of disciplined training and experience, with them to their new civilian lives. I thought Ben was no different.

I now smiled to myself as I momentarily imagined I had just signed on with Colonel Halley's militia and would be serving under his command as his financial officer. As the interview was complete, I stood up to leave, shook Ben's hand, and said, "Well, thanks for everything, Colonel. I'll see you soon in Tehran."

I immediately thought to myself, *Colonel? Did I really address Ben as Colonel? What was I thinking? I have to cut out the daydreaming and stay more focused on the important things that really matter!*

But he didn't seem to mind at all, and I believed he enjoyed hearing the sound of that word. I was just glad I didn't salute him!

The next thirty days was a whirlwind of activity as I took care of my personal business and tied up all the loose ends in preparation for leaving. I sold my vehicle along with most of my personal property and donated the rest to a thrift store. I then leased my house, rented a car, and moved into a small motel just down the street from Shell.

While packing, I didn't forget to bring along my rabbit's foot key chain, which was a good-luck charm that had served me well for years. I tossed it into one of my two heavy suitcases. Wheels had been around a long time, yet I had never seen them installed on any suitcase. I would have to carry them.

I was prepared to depart sooner, but the items holding up my journey were the receipt of my passport, my Iranian visa, and my residency permit. I subsequently received my expedited passport on August 8. I then turned it over to Shell personnel, along with my negative PPD skin test result, to be sent to Houston for the required Iranian stamps.

I then scheduled my flight through the Shell travel department for the seventeenth of August, which fell on a Wednesday. It was advisable for a new employee to depart on Wednesday, as the Iranian weekend was observed on Friday and Saturday. You would typically arrive in Tehran the next day on Thursday afternoon and would have the next two days off work to relax and deal with the exhausting jet lag. You would then report to work on Sunday morning for the beginning of the five-day workweek, which ended on Thursday.

Ramadan began on Tuesday, August 16. Shell didn't have an Iranian orientation class at that time, but when I processed through personnel, they advised me as a foreigner to keep a low profile and treat the religious holiday with the utmost respect.

I would be flying on an Eastern Airlines L-1011 Tristar wide-body aircraft from DFW near Dallas to JFK in New York. I would then connect with a Pan Am flight on a 747 jumbo for the almost thirteen-hour flight to Tehran's Mehrabad International Airport.

John Robert Tipton

While waiting in line to board the L-1011, I eavesdropped on the conversation two passengers behind me were having about Elvis Presley. He had just passed away the day before, and they were speculating about the cause of his untimely death. Elvis had died on the first day of Ramadan.

CHAPTER II

I arrived at Mehrabad late Thursday afternoon as scheduled and was met by Ben inside the terminal building after I had processed through customs. We hurried through the terminal as Ben had Albert, one of Shell's three Iranian contract drivers, waiting outside and parked in a passenger-loading zone.

We then drove to my temporary lodging at the Intercontinental Hotel downtown where Ben dropped me off at the lobby. Shell would provide accommodations for up to thirty days in a hotel before I would have to move to permanent housing. Albert informed me that he would be picking me up on Sunday morning at about seven-thirty to take me to work.

I spent my first weekend exploring my new environs. Just about everything was foreign to me, including the people, their dress, language, food, alphabet, vehicles, buildings, and even sidewalks. I felt like a fish out of water that had just been tossed onto the shore of a strange new land I knew nothing about. I did my best to resist the xenophobic urge to return to the secure, familiar surroundings of my hotel room and stay there. My first experience with jet lag then kicked in, and I found myself unable to sleep at night or stay awake during the middle of the afternoon.

I was glad when Sunday morning rolled around. Albert picked me up at the hotel and dropped me off on Sepahbod Zahedi Street in front of our office building. I entered through the green-tinted, double-glassed doors into the lobby. It looked quite inviting with its shiny white marble floor and polished mahogany furnishings that matched the interior mahogany doors.

Our street, Sepahbod Zahedi, was named in honor of Fazlollah Zahedi. He was an Iranian general and statesman who previously served the country as prime minister.

I could see a desk at the opposite wall manned by two uniformed Iranian air force military policemen. Hanging on the wall just above their heads was a large gilded frame holding a photograph of Mohammad Reza Pahlavi, the Shah (king) of Iran. He was wearing a military dress uniform decorated with ribbons and metals. I had noticed similar pictures of the Shah, sometimes including his family, prominently displayed in all commercial storefront businesses.

The Shah was the constitutional monarch of Iran since replacing his father on the throne in 1941. Using his oil-generated wealth, he had modernized his country and allied himself with the West. Iran, whose name was Persia until changed in 1935, was considered one of America's most important and closest allies in the region. The two names Iran and Persia can be used interchangeably.

I then presented my Shell Helicopter picture badge to the guards. With a subtle wave, I was motioned up the stairway to the left. Ben had already arrived, and I met him in his rear-corner office on the second floor. He then introduced me to his newly hired secretary, Mary Mannelli, whose desk was located just outside of Ben's office.

Mary was an attractive young lady of Italian decent. She was in her midtwenties and had long, brown hair that flowed over her shoulders. She was from the Jersey Shore and had accompanied her husband to Iran. He was a helicopter pilot who worked for an oil service company in the southern oil fields and was absent from home for weeks at a time. Mary wanted to work to be able to get out of the house and have something to occupy her time. I could tell Ben was pleased to have Mary working in our office.

Ben then took me on a tour of the second floor and showed me the office I had been assigned. It was the corner office in the front of the building directly above the stairway to nowhere. I was pleased my new office had a window that looked out onto Sepahbod Zahedi Street and a portion of downtown. It was sparsely furnished with a desk, a swivel armchair, and a four-drawer filing cabinet. I then made a mental note to requisition a couple of chairs and a small safe for the petty cash fund that I would administer.

John in his corner office

We then walked up to the largely vacant third floor, and Ben explained where we would be constructing the cafeteria, the kitchen, and the executive dining room. From there, we proceeded down to the ground floor and checked out the area where the media room would be built.

15

I spent the first week just trying to get settled in at work and attempting to get my personal life into some semblance of order. I was relieved the workweek was over when I arrived back at the hotel on Thursday afternoon. I already had my Friday planned with a visit to the Tehran Grand Bazaar located south of the office on Ferdosi Avenue. This street was named to honor Hakim Ferdosi Tusi who was famously known as Ferdosi, the great Persian poet.

When I arrived at my hotel room, I put the key into the door lock and jiggled the handle back and forth as I attempted to open the door.

What? What's wrong with this key? I thought to myself. *Maybe this door lock is broken or something.*

I then took the elevator down to the lobby and explained my key problem to the front desk clerk.

In response, he firmly said, "Mr. Tipton, your stay with us has now exceeded your reservation. You had a reservation for one week, and this is your eighth day in this hotel. You must return to your room, pack your bags, and check out of the hotel. Your room has already been assigned to someone with a confirmed reservation, and he is now patiently waiting in the lobby for you to depart." He then handed me a room key that would open my door.

I couldn't believe what this idiot desk clerk had just told me, and I knew that it must be a mistake. Ben had told me upon my arrival I would be staying at the Intercontinental Hotel for the entire month.

I located a pay phone in the lobby and dialed Ben's home number. I had earlier written it down on a piece of paper and carried it in my wallet for just such an emergency.

When he answered I said, "Sir, you're not going to believe this, but I just got tossed out of the hotel. They said my stay had exceeded my reservation."

Ben replied, "Yeah, I was afraid this might happen. Amir has been lobbying the Intercontinental to extend your reservation. We were only able to get a one-week reservation for you, and I did not know until you called tonight that we were unsuccessful with getting it extended. I would have told you about this earlier, but I just didn't want to worry you unnecessarily about something that might not happen at all."

Amir was Shell's Iranian public affairs employee. When Ben interviewed him, Amir emphasized his influential family and political connections as qualifications for the job. Every Western company that did business in Iran needed a knowledgeable, Farsi-speaking employee who was able to deal with the government bureaucracy and cut through the official red tape.

However, I couldn't help but doubt Amir was really that connected if he was unable to get my hotel reservation extended. It seemed like a simple-enough task, but in reality, there were few hotel rooms available in Tehran.

Tehran was a large metropolitan city populated by millions with only three major chain hotels. The oil boom of the seventies coupled with the Shah's industrialization plans resulted in an economic expansion that quickly filled the city's hotel rooms to capacity. Shell would later solve this problem by leasing a four-bedroom villa that would double as TDY (temporary duty) housing and as an employee recreation center.

I was tempted to explain to Ben that he should give me the heads-up on anything affecting my personal well-being, such as getting tossed out of the hotel for lack of a reservation. But I wisely kept my mouth shut, as I knew Ben well enough by now to know he was not about to leave his financial officer homeless on the streets of downtown Tehran. I already suspected he had my back as he explained the situation.

"Since Amir tells me there is not another available hotel room in all of Tehran, I would like to invite you to stay with my wife Shirley and me," he said. "We have a three-bedroom villa in north Tehran. There's lots of room, and you are welcome to stay here until you locate your permanent housing."

I enthusiastically replied, "Hey thanks, sir. That's great. Leave the light on, and I'll be right over!"

Ben then gave me the address and said that I would have to take a taxi. He did not own a personal vehicle, as he had wisely refused to drive in the Tehran traffic. He depended on the Shell contract drivers for his transportation, but they had already gone home for the day. However, this was not a problem, as there were usually several taxis waiting just outside the hotel for a fare.

Ben and Shirley had a beautiful, newly built, free-standing villa in one of the nicer neighborhoods in north Tehran. It was professionally landscaped with an inviting swimming pool and completely surrounded by a garden wall. This company-furnished housing provided Ben a needed escape from the urban environment.

While I appreciated the help, and Ben and Shirley were the most gracious hosts, I knew I soon needed to find a place of my own. The housing market was overheated, like the hotel accommodations, and finding an acceptable place was not an easy task.

There were realtors who would assist you in finding a rental, but they usually charged a fee equal to half of the first month's rent and sometimes more. It was customary for this fee to be paid by the renter, and the landlord would pay nothing. I didn't care for this arrangement and hoped I would be able to find a place on my own.

Tehran had a newspaper, the *Daily Kayhan*, which published both English and Farsi editions. I began to watch the classified ads in the English edition for available apartments.

I soon came across an ad for a one-bedroom, furnished apartment on Nilufar Street, which was in a residential area just north of downtown. *Nilufar* translated as "water lily" and was also a female given name. This apartment was unusual, because it was a furnished one-bedroom. Most available apartments had either two or three bedrooms, and none were furnished. It was also attractively priced within my housing allowance.

I gave the landlord a call and made an appointment to see the apartment. It was in a typical flat-roofed, three-story building with balconies across the front and one apartment on each floor. The first two floors had two-bedroom apartments, and there was a one-bedroom unit the same size on the third floor for rent. Mohammad, the landlord, was the aging patriarch of his extended family that occupied the first two floors. The family had originally occupied the entire building but had vacated the top floor for the economy of the rental income.

The apartment was sparsely furnished with the furniture they had left behind, but it would be enough. It had a spacious living/dining room area with a separate bedroom, kitchen, and bathroom.

The kitchen came equipped with a small refrigerator and a cook stove attached to a five-gallon propane tank. There was also a washer and dryer in the kitchen, but Mohammad explained that the dryer was unusable, as there was not enough electric power coming into the apartment to run it. He then showed me the retractable clothesline he had installed across the balcony. I would dry my clothes like everyone else—by hanging them across the balcony.

This apartment was heated with kerosene and had a black metal kerosene heater in the living room that was vented through the outside wall. For cooling there was an evaporative cooler on the roof that circulated cooled humid air throughout the ceiling duct system. The high, dry climate of Tehran was perfect for swamp coolers, and they were visible on most flat roofs. Air conditioners were rarely used in private residences.

*Tehran's flat roofs and swamp coolers with Mount Tochal
(elevation 13,005 feet) in the background*

I asked for a six-month lease, as I wasn't sure how long I wanted to stay at this location. I moved in three days later after signing a standard lease document for a rental term of six months written in both English and Farsi.

Mohammad then invited me to dinner on the first floor where I was introduced to his entire family. As I arrived, I removed my shoes and left them outside the front door before entering their residence. It was their practice for everyone to leave their dusty shoes outside the home's entryway. With typical Persian hospitality, the entire family extended their warm welcome to me. They did their best to make me feel right at home, and I was treated like one of the family.

Looking east on Nilufar Street from my third-story balcony

As I settled into my new dwelling, I soon learned about my responsibilities as a tenant in regard to the *baarf* (snow) removal, the *ashgal* (garbage) collection, and the *naft* (kerosene) delivery. It was customary in Iran for the occupant of the top floor of an apartment building to have the responsibility for removal of snow off the flat roof during the winter months. Mohammad said he would hire a *baarfee* for the snow removal as needed, but I would have to pay for it. In addition, the *ashgal* was picked up once a week on Tuesday by the *ashgalee* at curbside in front of the building.

As the weather cooled off and summer changed to fall, *naft* was delivered by the *naftee* in a small tanker on a weekly basis. Every week I would leave two twenty-liter red plastic containers on the curb in front of our building to be filled. As I was usually at work, Mohammad would pay for the *naft*, and I would in return reimburse him.

I would then carry the containers one at a time up the stairs to the third floor and usually empty one of them into an opening in the top of the heater. To light the heater you simply had to drop a lighted match through the same opening in the top, and it fell into the reservoir at the bottom. There was always the sound of a small explosion and then you could feel the welcome heat a short time later.

But my heater was not properly sealed, and there was always the faint smell of *naft* that permeated the entire apartment. Also, when dusting, I always noticed a thin film of black soot along with the fine dust that would settle on everything. This even affected my attire, as I noticed my white clothing had now turned to a light shade of gray. I couldn't help but wonder how my health would be adversely affected by having to breathe this stuff.

Most residences in Tehran used this same type of heating, which contributed significantly to the smog and soot in the air. The particles of soot would settle on the outside of buildings, giving the city a sort of gritty feel. Even the new construction was not exempt and seemed to age prematurely.

It seemed that most of Tehran was under construction with an industrialization-fueled building boom. In some areas you could see construction cranes as far as the eye could see. There was some urban humor going around that stated the construction crane was the national bird of Iran.

The typical construction method used for most of the larger buildings employed the usual steel-beam supporting framework. The walls and floors between the steel beams were then constructed using red-clay bricks. The brick floors had to be arched in order to be supportive, and the surface was then evened out on both sides with masonry. I worried about how these arched brick floors would fare during an earthquake, because I believed our office building was constructed using the same technique.

I noticed that some buildings appeared to be complete except for the unsightly rebar left protruding out of the flat roofs where the vertical structural columns were located. This made it appear there would be another floor added to the existing structure. When I asked about this, I was informed that these buildings were considered unfinished by the taxing authority and were therefore not subject to property taxes until completed someday in the future.

Once I had gotten the housing issue out of the way, I had to find my own vehicle, as transportation in Tehran was mostly car-dependent. Local public transportation was difficult and confusing for a foreigner. The city had green double-decker buses in the downtown area, but the schedules and route information were written only in Farsi. I wasn't about to board one of these buses without knowing in advance where it was going or when it was returning.

There were call cabs available, but calling one was usually made difficult due to the language barrier. In addition, there were the shared orange taxis that held up to four passengers and filled the streets of downtown. To get one of these taxis to stop, you had to stand on the curb and shout out your destination as the taxi passed by. If the taxi driver was going your way, then the he just might stop for you.

Most of the orange taxis were Paykons, which was the only passenger vehicle totally designed and manufactured in Iran. The imported vehicles were expensive as they heavily taxed, but the Paykon was affordable to many people. It was a small, dependable car that could snugly hold a driver and four passengers. In addition, it was economical to drive and could be easily repaired by most mechanics. It was a popular automobile, as most vehicles on the streets seemed to be Paykons. The shared taxis received the name of orange taxis, as their bodies were painted a bright orange with the roofs painted white to reflect the heat.

Transportation to and from work was provided by Shell as an expatriate employee benefit. Each morning I would be picked up by one of the contract drivers, usually along with three other employees who filled the small vehicle to its capacity. During the afternoon after work, we would be taken home by the same driver but in the reverse order of arriving. It reminded me of my carpooling days in Dallas. But other than using this company-provided transportation, I found it easier to walk everywhere, because I was uncomfortable using the public transportation services.

The traffic in downtown Tehran would definitely try your patience. Rush hour began early and lasted all day without a pause. The bad driving habits of others were so commonplace it seemed to be the normal way to drive. It appeared many people lost their cultural politeness when they got behind the wheel and became anonymous in the frustrating traffic.

Tempers sometimes flared. On two different occasions while riding in a call cab, my driver had a dispute with another driver. They both pulled over to the curb and quickly exited their vehicles. While flailing their arms about, the two men then had a heated discussion in Farsi that I could not comprehend. Just as I was convinced they were about to come to blows, the quarrel was somehow settled. My taxi driver then peacefully drove away while noticeably mumbling something under his breath.

But even though the traffic was a dangerous headache, I still wanted the freedom of having my own personal transportation. I began to watch the classified ads in the English edition of the *Daily Kahan* newspaper for a gently used Paykon. I recognized that this car offered the best value for a personal vehicle in terms of price, maintenance, and utility.

It was in the paper that I first noticed the advertisement for the jeep. I read it with interest and then dismissed it as I remembered I was in the market for a used Paykon. But two days later the ad caught my attention again. This time I called the owner, and he brought the jeep to my office building and parked it outside on the street.

It was a restored 1955 Jeep model CJ-5. The body was in good shape with no dents or rust, the canvas top and doors were in good condition, and the tires were new. It had a recent orange paint job, which was the same color as the orange taxis. I realized it was an old vehicle, but I had worked on old cars before and thought I could keep it running even in Tehran. I also thought a jeep would get some respect in the Tehran traffic. It ran well and looked great, and I was tempted to buy it. I then kicked the tires, took it for a test drive, and even tried out the stock horn.

The sound of automobile horns was ever present, as many drivers tended to use their horns regularly in the traffic. There almost seemed to be a competition among the drivers to see who had the most obnoxious horn. The horn that played "The Call to the Post" was common. This is the familiar bugle call that is played before horse races. An excerpt from the "Boogie Woogie Bugle Boy" was right up there in popularity. I always thought the most amusing horn was the one that would play the first eleven notes of "Dixie," though few in Tehran would know the significance of that song.

There was one horn I never once heard in Tehran—the ahooga horn first used on the Ford Model T and then later on submarines as a dive horn. I needed this horn so I could join the obnoxious-horn competition. I had one shipped in my first care package from Fort Worth. I then installed it on my jeep and usually managed to get some attention and a little respect whenever I used it.

After the test drive, I agreed to buy the jeep and had to transfer the title to my name. Traffic police in Tehran had the authority to write moving traffic violations against the vehicle instead of the driver. If they witnessed a moving-traffic offence, the policeman could simply write a ticket against the license plate number of the vehicle. The owner would be unaware of the infraction until the vehicle was sold and the title transferred to a new owner. At that time, any unpaid tickets on file would have to be paid by either the buyer or the seller.

My CJ-5 Jeep with the Alborz mountain range in the background

To deal with the bureaucracy and the language barrier, I asked Freda at the office to help me transfer the title to my name. Freda did secretarial work and was always agreeable to assist the American employees with translation or official matters. If you needed help with a lease, a driver's license, a car title, or any other official document, you could always depend on Freda. She was in her midtwenties and had beautiful olive-colored skin, sparkling greenish eyes, and short dark hair with bangs hanging across her forehead. She always had a smile on her face and soon became everyone's favorite in the office. Freda was fluent in English and spoke with a British accent. She had never been to England, but her English teacher was British. Freda was married without children.

Freda always dressed conservatively, wearing Western-styled clothing that would completely cover both her arms and legs. She never wore a headscarf at work but did wear a black chador in public whenever she left the office. Chadors came in several different subdued colors and sometimes subtle patterns, but the color black was traditional for married women. They were worn in public but typically not inside the home.

Everyone needed Freda's help at one time or another, and she was always willing to lend a hand. With her assistance, I was able to transfer the title to my name; fortunately, there were no unpaid tickets issued against the jeep.

At work we received the engineering drawings and specifications for the construction of the cafeteria and kitchen, the executive dining room, and the media room. We obtained competitive bids from three local construction companies recommended by the Iranian air force, and construction activity was underway. The stainless-steel kitchen equipment, cafeteria furnishings, and media equipment were being imported from Fort Worth and had already been shipped. The heavily carved rococo furnishings the generals preferred for their executive dining room would be purchased locally.

Construction activity was also underway in Isfahan for our helicopter-manufacturing facility. A British international construction company was contracted by Shell in Fort Worth to accomplish the work. The targeted completion date was estimated to be two-plus years.

Shell employees were now beginning to trickle into Tehran on their way to Isfahan. We took turns meeting them at the airport and making sure that they were safely in a hotel room or Shell TDY housing for the night. Transportation to the airport the next morning was arranged for the Iran Air flight to Isfahan.

Our office was now fully staffed with the six Shell managers who would interface with the appropriate Iranian generals. As manager of finance I would be responsible for providing support to General Ghorbani, who handled the financial matters for Sauzi Helicopter Iran.

General Ghorbani was a soft-spoken, balding man just past middle age. You could tell by his mild-mannered demeanor that he had made it to the top. He always welcomed me into his office with a warm smile and a firm handshake. Then there would be the traditional small cup of sweetened tea offered along with an Iranian delicacy, such as smoked almonds, pickled walnuts, or stuffed dates. I always gracefully accepted his hospitality, having learned from our contract drivers that sharing was an important part of the Iranian culture. I knew it would have been rude of me to refuse his generosity. During this time, there was always some friendly small talk before we finished with our ritual and got down to business.

In the back of my mind, I had never forgotten what Ray Cole mentioned in Fort Worth about the quarterly contract payments and Shell's bottom line. I was dreading the day when I would have to remind General Ghorbani about a past-due payment. Fortunately, the payment was always processed in a timely manner, and it never became an issue.

There were three Iranian drivers who were contracted by Shell to provide company transportation. This included transportation to and from work for the employees and use of the vehicles for company business during the day. Each drove a Paykon, which would be parked in the basement during the workday when not in use.

There was a small room adjacent to the parking area in the basement that was assigned to the drivers. They would wait in this room, usually reading newspapers and eating something, until their services were needed. I learned about the Iranian tradition of sharing food, as they would never let me say no when they offered to share whatever they were eating. I soon realized that these guys had probably never met a stranger, and they quickly befriended me.

It was during December I first noticed the cut pine trees on the sidewalk leaning against the side of a building downtown. I just couldn't imagine why they were selling pine trees in Tehran until I remembered that Christmas was soon approaching. These weren't the manicured nursery-grown trees you could buy at home but were the short-leaf desert pines that thrived in the valleys outside Tehran. It didn't seem to matter, though, as they sold briskly, and within a few days, the Christmas trees disappeared.

In celebration of the holiday, we had a company-sponsored office Christmas party. The only area available for the party on the second floor was the small entrance area just outside the elevator. There was hardly enough room for the Christmas tree, the table filled with holiday food, and the attendees who gathered around. We cordially invited the generals and their civilian staff to join us in our celebration. Some of their staff attended, but all of the generals were conspicuous by their absence.

Office Christmas party

On December 31, 1977, President Jimmy Carter and First Lady Rosaline made a state visit to Tehran. They were met at the Mehrabad Airport by the Shah and his wife, Empress Farah. There was then a motorcade that passed through the streets of downtown on their way to a New Year's Eve state dinner at Niavaran Palace in northern Tehran.

The streets were decked out with American and Iranian flags, and the sidewalks were crowded with approving Iranian people. There were welcoming banners hanging along the motorcade route, and the color scheme for the visit was definitely red, white, and blue.

I conspicuously watched the motorcade from a mostly vacant street corner on the edge of downtown in hopes that both the Shah and the president would notice and acknowledge my presence. I eagerly waved a large American flag that I had earlier purchased from a street vendor. As the royal motorcade passed by in front of me, both the president and the shah noticed my flag waving and politely smiled while returning my wave.

During a televised toast that night at the state dinner, President Carter said, "Under the Shah's brilliant leadership, Iran is an island of stability in one of the most troublesome regions of the world. There is no other state figure whom I could appreciate and like more."

The two leaders would never meet again.

Within weeks of President Carter's visit, a series of protests denouncing the Shah's regime broke out in the religious city of Qom located southeast of Tehran. As foreigners, we never heard about these protests in the media, primarily due to our lack of available information. I never saw the protests reported in the English-language *Daily Kayhan* newspaper, but we did hear about them at work from Freda. However, she didn't seem too concerned about it, so it didn't worry me either. None of us had a clue that the seeds of the Iranian Revolution had sprouted.

It could be argued, however, that the Iranian Revolution actually began years earlier. During the early sixties, there was an Islamic scholar who clashed with the Shah's government over its policies concerning the unequal distribution of wealth and the westernization of Iran. His name was the Ayatollah Ruhollah Khomeini. The Shah's government resolved the difficulty by banishing him to Iraq to go into exile during 1963. Some thought that year marked the beginning of the revolution. Iraq, under pressure from the Iranian government, would later expel the Ayatollah, and he would seek refuge in Paris.

There were uncensored American newspapers and weekly news magazines available at the newsstands. But because of the distance and time in customs clearance, they were almost a week old by the time they hit the newsstands. Nothing is worse than reading week-old news, so many English-speaking foreigners relied on the hourly BBC shortwave news broadcast from London for current world news. After Freda informed me about the protests, I tuned in to the BBC but did not hear any coverage on the unrest in Qom.

At work we primarily relied on the international telephone lines and the weekly DHL pouch for communication with Fort Worth. The company also rented a post-office box at the downtown Iranian PTT (postal, telephone, and telegraph) for both business and personal employee mail. In addition, when Shell employees traveled back and forth, they usually acted as couriers, delivering company correspondence and information as needed.

There was no English television or radio broadcast in Tehran. However, there was American programming available on television that was dubbed in Farsi without English subtitles. Freda's favorite American show was *The Waltons*. She laughingly started calling me John-Boy at work, and others picked it up. She said I didn't look like John-Boy Walton, but I shared some of his mannerisms.

Shortly after arriving in Tehran, I realized the importance of learning Farsi, as most Iranians I came in contact with on a day-to-day basis did not speak English.

Shell encouraged this by paying for the classes. I soon found myself taking my first Farsi class at the Iran-American Society's Cultural Center in the northern part of the city.

I found it very difficult attempting to learn a new language I could neither read nor write. The Farsi language also had new sounds and inflections that were completely foreign to my Western ear. But it gradually got easier, as I would use the English alphabet to phonetically memorize and practice saying a word, a phrase, or even an entire sentence.

I then worked up the courage to go out on the street and ask non-English-speaking Iranians questions I had memorized. These were simple questions concerning perhaps a price, the time, or the location of a street or building. Each question was always prefaced with the same two words: *bebacksheed agaha* (excuse me, mister).

I knew I was successful if it was understood what I had said, although I could rarely understand the answer. Sometimes they would recognize me as being an American and answer in English, which didn't help things at all. But the most important thing was I had actually begun speaking this language to others.

I continued to practice, took a second Farsi class, and, with more difficulty, memorized the alphabet and gradually learned to read and write a few words. With a lot of work, I eventually found I could say almost anything I wanted in Farsi, although in a very elementary manner, much as a young child would speak. But this level of competence was enough to communicate with others, and I knew I didn't necessarily need fluency. I did, however, continue to expand my Farsi by adding new words and phrases to my vocabulary.

But there was more to Farsi than just learning the spoken word. I always thought of their clever communication of the unspoken word *no*, as the Iranian degrees of the silent no.

As Americans, we convey this unspoken negative word by simply moving our heads from side to side. This means definitely no; there is nothing subtle about it, and it can't be easily concealed from others.

But with the Iranians it was much more complex. They communicated their most discrete no by simply closing their eyes and then opening them after a slight pause. It was a gentle, personal no to be seen and understood only by the recipient.

The next, more assertive no was indicated by an upward movement of the head. This upward movement could be significant or so slight it would hardly be noticed by others. The head movement could be gently combined with the closed eyes to make that no slightly more definite.

The next level of no was communicated with a clicking sound made by pressing your tongue against the top of your mouth and then quickly releasing it as you draw air in. The loudness of this click, and/or the number of clicks, indicated the level of its assertiveness.

The final, most definite no was communicated by combining the upward head movement with the clicking sound. The more pronounced the head movement and the louder the click(s) indicated the most definite no.

So with a little practice, I learned their system of communicating the unspoken word no and easily fell into the habit of using it instead of shaking my head from side to side. At work, I introduced this to my colleagues, and some fell into the practice of using the clicking sound and head movement themselves.

The Persians liked to borrow words from the French. In Farsi, elevator was *ascenseaur*, furniture was *meubles*, and croissant was croissant. But the French word used in everyday conversation was *merci*. The Farsi word for thank you was *motshakaram*, which does not easily roll off the tongue. *Merci* seemed to be a far easier substitute, and I soon routinely began using this word myself.

The people of Iran are a handsome mixture that was partly the result of the repeated invasions of long ago. Most have dark features, but it wasn't unusual to see an occasional fair-skinned, blue-eyed blonde or sometimes even a Lucy redhead. Some Persians, influenced by the genetic pool left behind by the Genghis Kahn invasion, looked as though they had just arrived from the steps of Mongolia. There was definitely an Oriental influence in their diversity.

Alcohol was readily available in Iran. The Iranians made their own wine, distilled their own vodka, and brewed their own *abjo*. In Farsi, *ab* means water, and *jo* means barley, which translates in English as barley water or beer. However, the other spirituous beverages were imported and quite expensive. In addition, there were no Western-style bars, nightclubs, or liquor stores, but the larger hotels did offer full-service bars to their guests and the general public.

Tehran is located on the foothills slopes of the east-west Alborz mountain range and extends southward to the central desert. Because Tehran is on the southern slope, you could always determine your directions as if you were using a compass. Uphill was always north, and downhill was always south. It was then a simple matter to determine east-west directions. I did notice that my ears would have to adjust to the changing air pressure as the elevation changed while driving in a north-south direction. Tehran is a huge, sprawling city, but I never completely lost my way thanks to its convenient natural topography.

The city had been developed up the northern slopes to the highest elevations possible. If you wanted to go mountain hiking, you only had to drive up to one of the northernmost neighborhoods and park on a residential street. The mountain trails began there on the edge of the suburban areas, and it was only a walk across the street to access them.

The hiking trails were constructed of asphalt with steps and handrails on the steeper terrain. As you're hiking up, you're never able to see the top of the mountain. You can only see upward as far as the next level. When you got to that level, then you could only see the next higher level, and this seemed to go on forever. I was always confident I would be able to hike to the trail's end but never once made it. The 180-degree panoramic view of Tehran from this vantage point on a clear day was nothing short of breathtaking.

Author taking a hike in north Tehran

By mid-January, the mountains overlooking Tehran were completely covered with a heavy layer of white powder and were truly spectacular when you could see them. They were usually visible during the first part of the morning, but by midmorning they would usually be completely obscured by the heavy smog.

The humid airflow from the Caspian Sea just north of Tehran is blocked by the east-west mountain range that has peaks extending upward to more than eighteen thousand feet at the highest elevation. North of the mountains the rainfall is plentiful, and there are low-hanging clouds, lush vegetation, and even rice paddies.

On the arid Tehran side, there is commonly a thermal inversion created by the lack of airflow over the mountains, which all too often traps Tehran's polluted air. Upper respiratory problems were not uncommon due to the airborne pollutants.

Sepahbod Zahedi Street on a clear day

Sepahbod Zahedi Street on a smoggy day.

There were two ski resorts in the mountains about an hour's drive northeast of Tehran. The Shah was known to be an avid snow skier, and both the Dizin and Shemshak Resorts were conveniently located nearby his Niavaran Palace in north Tehran.

I had been skiing several times at the resorts in New Mexico and had taken ski lessons while there. I wanted to go skiing while in Iran and chose to go to the Shemshak Resort, as it was nearer to Tehran than Dizin. Little did I know, Shemshak catered primarily to advanced skiers, while the Dizin Resort was designed for the beginner and intermediate skier.

It was a beautiful drive to Shemshak up the winding two-lane asphalt road with green lakes nestled among spectacular snow-covered mountains. These mountains were mostly treeless with trees being limited to stream banks and the valley floors. Before reaching Shemshack, the asphalt road turned to gravel, and the resort suddenly came into view as I drove down into the ski basin from above.

Alborz Mountain view north of Tehran

Shemshak had two main ski slopes coming down from the summit, and both were served by one chairlift. In addition, there were several smaller, individual lifts that serviced the gentler slopes at the lower elevations.

I rented some ski equipment and chose to ski at the lower level. I soon noticed a Shell Huey Viper Helicopter land on the relatively flat area adjacent to the chairlift. This was an army utility transport-type helicopter painted olive drab with Iranian army insignia. I had noticed it earlier, as it would land at the chairlift and then wait for maybe half an hour or so before flying upward toward the summit. It would then fly out of sight over the topmost ridge to where I couldn't see if it had landed above. In a few minutes, the helicopter would then return to the flat area near the chairlift and land again.

This had been going on for most of the morning, and my curiosity had gotten the best of me. I then skied down to the chairlift area after the helicopter landed and waited. I didn't have to wait long before I saw a party of five skiers coming down the moguled expert slope to the waiting helicopter. From their pictures, I recognized the Shah and his son, Crown Prince Reza. The group then boarded the helicopter, and it quickly took off again, heading back toward the summit. The Shah and his ski party were avoiding the lift line by using an army helicopter instead.

CHAPTER III

It felt good to leave the cold crisp, mountains and return to the high, balmy climate of Tehran. Thus far, it had been a mild winter with little snowfall in the city.

I knew the six-month lease for my apartment on *Nilufar* was expiring soon, and I wanted to find a new place within walking distance from the office. I started looking on the east-west residential streets north of the office and noticed an apartment for rent near *Kalantary Ponge* (Police Station 5). This police substation was also used as a staging area for the army troops assigned to the downtown area.

The apartment building was similar to the one on *Nilufar* with a balcony across the front, except it was larger and had a secured entry foyer. It was on the top floor, which meant I would continue to have the responsibility for snow removal off the flat roof. But more importantly, I would no longer have to deal with a naft heater, as this building had radiator-type heating that utilized a naft-fueled boiler in the basement.

But I now realized the snow-removal responsibility didn't seem to matter much at all. The winter of 1978 in Tehran had been mild with practically no snowfall in the city. I never once had to pay for snow removal off my apartment building's roof during the entire winter. It was if the climate had somehow changed.

The apartment was spacious with a living and dining room, two bedrooms, kitchen, bathroom, and a large no room. The no room was a large entry room adjacent to the living room that seemingly served no purpose to most Westerners and was appropriately called the no room.

I would have to completely furnish the new apartment, but I wasn't too concerned, as I now hoped to stay in Tehran for the duration of the contract, which could be for years. I had gradually grown comfortable with the Iranian culture and living among the Iranian people. I now knew I could live in Tehran for the long term. I signed a one-year lease and moved into my new home just before the beginning of *Nowruz* (New Year) in March.

I also realized I had developed feelings for Freda. However, she was a married woman, and I knew I couldn't get myself involved with someone like that. I had suppressed these feelings, but nonetheless, they were still with me. I could only imagine the penalties for such mischief, but I knew deep down inside, my heart was now in Iran.

Shortly after moving into my new apartment, I noticed white smoke rising upward from the generally quiet street below. It was a Tuesday evening at about twilight. I went out on my front balcony to get a better look and was amazed to see my Persian neighbors building bonfires up and down the middle of the street about every block or so.

As the bonfires heated up and the flames grew higher, both children and adults alike begin jumping over the fires after first getting a running start. It was a festive time with the family, filled with laughter and merriment as they jumped over the flames. As darkness arrived, the fires were allowed to burn down to ashes, and the people went back inside their homes. Traffic then resumed, and things returned to normal. I thought at the time this custom probably had something to do with Nowruz. Perhaps they were somehow saying good-bye to the old year and welcoming the new.

The next day at work I asked Freda about the bonfire jumping, and she said it was a festival of light known as *Chaharshanbe Souri*, which translates in English as Red Wednesday. By jumping over the fires, the participant returns his tired, yellow essence to the flames and reinvigorates himself by taking on the red. It marked the beginning of the Nowruz celebrations on the eve of the last Wednesday of the Persian year. Freda described it as a celebration of light, which represented good, triumphing over darkness, which represented bad.

Nowruz, the Persian New Year, is the most important holiday in Iran. It occurs on the first day of spring at the exact time of the vernal equinox when night and day are equal in length; the holiday lasts for a month. It is a time of renewal with spring house cleaning, new clothing for the family, special holiday foods, gift exchanges, and visits with family and friends.

I had been in-country for more than six months and had earned my first week of R&R. I booked a flight with Iran Air from Tehran to Kabul and scheduled my return during the first week of Nowruz. This New Year holiday is also celebrated in Afghanistan.

The flight left as scheduled but made an unscheduled landing at Kandahar Airfield. The Kabul International Airport had closed due to poor visibility caused by heavy fog that developed as our flight was en route. The Kandahar airport had a modern appearance with a large terminal building. It had been built by the Americans in the early sixties and was now mostly vacant with little or no activity. Our airplane was the only commercial aircraft I observed at the entire airport.

All the passengers were instructed to deplane down the stairway onto the tarmac and were met by the Iran Air captain. He announced that the flight was returning to Tehran, and that any passengers who wanted to return with him could do so. He added that the passengers who chose to stay were no longer the responsibility of Iran Air and would have to arrange their own transportation to Kabul.

Most passengers chose to stay without knowing how they would get to Kabul, which was almost three hundred miles away. The passengers then had to climb into the luggage compartment of the aircraft to unload and sort out the luggage as there were no baggage handlers at the airport.

Passengers unloading their luggage from Iran Air aircraft at Kandahar Airfield

Because there was no available telephone service or public transportation, the airport personnel in the control tower radioed the Kabul International Airport requesting a bus to transport the passengers to Kabul. The bus finally arrived about eight hours later, and we departed Kandahar around midnight.

The bus ride was an adventure in itself. It was an old bus with a busted-out window in the front and a broken rear door at the back that could not be completely closed. This created a freezing-cold, dusty draft that whistled through the entire length of the bus. As we traveled through a heavy dust storm, I watched my olive-green field jacket turn a light shade of brown. The bus driver provided drinking water with a galvanized container located in the middle of the aisle. There was a communal steel drinking cup attached for everyone's use. I was relieved when we finally arrived in Kabul about midmorning.

I didn't have hotel reservations, so I had a taxi driver take me to a downtown hotel. The driver drove me to a small rustic hotel on Chicken Street, which was in a touristy area populated by a large number of Western hippies. Chicken Street is located in a shopping area well known for its Afghani fur and leather handicrafts, wood carvings, carpet shops, and antique stores, which all catered mostly to foreigners.

Author in Kabul

It was now a time of relative peace and prosperity for Afghanistan, which was ruled by the monarchy of President Daoud Kahn. The peace, however, was soon to be shattered one month later by the coup that assassinated the president and overthrew his government. This coup preceded the Russian invasion less than one year later during December 1979.

I spent the week seeing the sights and browsing the shops of Kabul, eventually buying an old copper teapot and a hand-knotted Turkoman carpet. The little Farsi I knew came in handy, as many people in Kabul spoke this language. I also took a day trip on a tour bus to Bamiyan to see the giant Buddhas carved into the mountainside. I departed Kabul on Iran Air as scheduled and arrived safely back in Tehran on a totally uneventful flight.

Shahmama Buddhist Statue (thirty-five meters) carved into mountainside at Bamiyan

When I arrived home, Nowruz was still being celebrated, and Freda mentioned Picnic Day, which occurs on the thirteenth day of the New Year. She said the entire country shuts down, and everyone has a family picnic outside, usually in a park or the countryside. She added that this holiday is called *Sizdah Bedar*, which translates in English as getting rid of the thirteenth.

Some Persians believe thirteen is an unlucky number that can be cleansed by going outside and celebrating the day by having a picnic with family and friends.

I always knew the number thirteen was unlucky but never knew why. I now thought perhaps my superstition was somehow rooted with the Persian beliefs of long ago. I knew I wasn't going to have a picnic on this day and wondered how I was going to get rid of the thirteenth with all its bad luck.

The thirteenth day of the New Year fell on April 1, which was on a Saturday. I had the day off, as it was the last day of the week, and I wanted to witness Picnic Day for myself.

About noon I walked down to Parke Tehran, which was a large city park in the southern part of the city. It was wooded with wide sidewalks, park benches, picnic tables, water features, gardens, and grassy areas. As I entered the crowded park, I could see the grassy areas and park tables were mostly occupied with people having picnics.

Parke Tehran

I had brought along my new Canon SLR 35mm camera and hoped to get some good pictures. As it was a new camera, I had developed the habit of focusing the lens and framing a picture just for practice without necessarily releasing the shutter and taking a picture.

As I was walking down the sidewalk, I noticed an Iranian family near the end of the park sitting on the grass and having their picnic. I recognized three generations with a mother and father, two small children, and the grandparents. Both women were wearing black chadors, and the children were playing together on the grass. Without giving it much thought, I aimed the camera at the family and framed in a perfect Persian family portrait but did not take the picture.

The entire family saw this and thought I had taken their photograph without first asking permission. I realized I had offended the family as the enraged father swiftly approached me angrily shouting things in Farsi I could not understand. It was his responsibility to save face and keep the respect of his family by confronting me about my offensive behavior. A curious crowd of Iranian men quickly gathered around to see what the commotion was all about.

Surrounded by foreign strangers in a crowded park, I now felt all alone and threatened. It's uncertain times like this when you just want to retreat back to the warm, protective security of the womb and stay there!

In the heat of the moment, all my Farsi suddenly left me as I attempted to explain in English that I had not actually taken a picture. The father obviously didn't comprehend my explanation, but I now understood what he was saying as he held out his hand and demanded my camera. He was so angry I knew my camera was about to be smashed against the sidewalk, and there was nothing I could do about it.

I handed the camera to the father, and he briefly examined it. He then rewound the film and removed the film canister from the back of the camera. He kept the roll of film but calmly handed my camera back to me; the crisis was over.

I knew though that my subtle revenge would be sweet. Once the father had the film developed, he would then discover, much to his chagrin, that there was no picture of his family taken by the rude American.

I then walked home and was becoming noticeably hungry, as I had not eaten for the day. But I didn't feel like going to a restaurant after the confrontation in the park. I had a piece of *barbari* bread at home left over from the day before. I knew it was probably stale by now, but I thought I'd give it a try anyway. I put some pomegranate jam on it, and as I bit down on the hard, crusty bread, I suddenly felt the crown on my upper-left front tooth give way. I retrieved the crown and knew I would now have to find a dentist to cement it back in place. I'd had the crown for several years after injuring my tooth in a bicycle accident.

Barbari bread is a large, flat rectangular piece of golden bread almost an inch thick and more than a foot in length. It is scored lengthwise across the top. The bread has to be bought fresh every day at the bakery and consumed fresh, as it tended to harden overnight. Every neighborhood had a small bakery that produced only *barbari* bread. The bakeries were easy enough to locate by the crowd of customers waiting outside on the sidewalk for the hot bread to come out of the beehive-shaped, brick-lined oven. This subsidized bread was cheap and almost seemed free at an equivalent price of about ten cents. It was delicious, and I usually didn't mind the wait.

The next day at work I purposely gave Freda a big smile as I said good morning. She saw the gap in my front teeth and at first laughed out loud but then sympathetically asked, "Oh, John-Boy *joon! Che shodeh?* (What happened?) *Che shodeh?*" (*Joon*, when used after someone's name, indicates friendship.)

I replied, "Freda joon, you won't believe my *Sizdah Bedar*. First, I had this incredible confrontation in Parke Tehran over nothing, and then my crown came loose after I bit down on a hard piece of barbari bread. I need to find a dentist that can cement it back in place. I hope you know of a good one nearby in the downtown area."

She then said jokingly, "Well, it sounds like you should have gone on a picnic."

I laughed as I replied, "*Medonom, medonom.* (I know, I know.) I promise I'll do that next year."

She answered, "I do know of a dentist within walking distance of the office. I believe he speaks English, and his name is Dr. Ahmazadeh. He did some work for me a while back and seemed to be a proper dentist. Would you like for me to call his office and make an appointment for you?"

I nodded in appreciation and replied, "*Kaylee motshakaram karnome.* (Thank you very much, ma'am.) That would be great if you would do that for me."

Freda then called Dr. Ahmazadeh's office and made an appointment for me at two o'clock the following afternoon.

I arrived at the dental office promptly at two o'clock the next day, fully expecting him to honor my appointment as scheduled. As time passed in the small waiting room, it occurred to me that perhaps the dentist had adjusted his appointment schedule to accommodate the expected cultural tardiness of his patients. Many Iranians were habitually late for most appointments. If they showed up within thirty minutes of the appointed time, they then considered themselves as being on time. There was always a polite apology, usually blaming their lateness on the traffic.

After waiting more than a half hour to see the dentist, his assistant entered the waiting room and informed me in Farsi he was ready to see me. I followed her into the adjacent room and sat down in the dental chair. Dr. Ahmazadeh came in, and we exchanged social pleasantries. I then explained to him what had happened. "On Saturday I bit down on a piece of hard barbari bread, and my crown came loose. I just need for you to cement it back in place."

I handed him my crown, and he placed it snuggly back over my tooth. It seemed to fit just fine as he said, "This crown will never stay cemented in place any length of time. You need a dental post installed in your tooth to hold the crown. This is my recommendation, and it would be useless for me to even consider cementing your crown back on your existing tooth."

Little did I realize at the time that there was economic pressure at work in the task of repairing my tooth. There was little money involved in cementing my crown back on, but installing a dental post was quite expensive and profitable for the dentist.

As I sat in the dental chair with the light still shining in my eyes, I knew I had to make a decision. I just wanted my tooth repaired, so I agreed to have the dental post installed.

After installing the dental post, Dr. Ahmazadeh then attempted to fit my crown over the tooth. As the crown had been custom-made to fit my tooth without a post, there was then not enough room inside it to accommodate the post.

The dentist then held my crown up to the light in front of me and began drilling out the inside, enlarging it enough to fit over the dental post. He appeared to be in a hurry as I watched him drill right through the front of my crown. My beautiful, porcelain-fused-to-gold crown now had a large hole in it that he repaired with mismatched white filling material.

I was furious, but I didn't have any recourse other than to pay the bill and leave. As I left the dental office, I realized had I gone on a picnic and gotten rid of the thirteenth, I would have never bitten down on that hard piece of bread, and none of this bad luck would have happened.

I soon noticed that I became self-conscious about my flawed front tooth and found it even affected the quality of my smile. I promised myself I would never return to another Iranian dentist.

CHAPTER IV

I had been in-country now for over ten months and I had thus far managed to resist buying my first Persian carpet. I was quite taken by them and had done my share of window-shopping.

I first noticed the Persian carpets upon arrival at the front desk of the Intercontinental Hotel. There was a carpet shop just off the lobby, and the proprietor had a beautiful coral-colored silk Qom displayed on the wall behind the reception desk. There was a spotlight shining on it that caused the silk to almost shimmer in the bright light. After I settled into my room, I returned to the lobby first thing just to check out the carpets.

Most of the carpet shops were clustered near the Tehran Bazaar in the southern part of the city. Several of them employed a sales technique based on total trust that I had never seen before.

When the shop proprietor would observe you admiring a particular carpet, he would suggest you take it home and try it out on your floor. There was no deposit asked and nothing that required your signature. He would not even bother to ask for your name, address, or telephone number. If you liked the carpet, you could return to the shop and pay for it, or you could return the carpet if you decided against buying it. I fell for this sales gimmick more than once and would eventually buy several of the handmade carpets, preferring the ones made of wool with tribal designs.

I was also awestruck by Tehran's antique stores, which were filled with a plethora of very old antiquities. I particularly became interested in the ancient Persian pottery that was usually encrusted with the iridescent patina of the ages. There were several shops, also near the Tehran Bazaar, that specialized in porcelain pottery, and they employed a sales technique of their own.

When the shop owner would catch you peering into his window and visually admiring his display of pottery, he would step outside on the sidewalk and politely invite you into his store. He would then sit you down at a table and offer you the traditional small cup of sweetened tea. After some small talk, the dealer would then present you, one at a time, with a collection of five or six pieces of museum-quality porcelain pottery in pristine condition. Plates and bowls were common, but jugs, beakers, jars, and spouted vessels were also available. Some were in the form of animals, and most were made with a high degree of craftsmanship. Others were so delicate that when held up to the light, you could see the ancient Persian designs subtly etched into the thin, translucent walls.

The dealer priced each piece individually and would then offer a better price if you bought the entire collection. Surprisingly, the pottery was not actually that expensive. I had previously noticed that when I left the country there were no questions in customs concerning Persian antiquities or cultural property. Even in Afghanistan, I encountered an issue in customs as to whether I would be allowed to take my antique teapot out of the country. It seemed to me the Iranians were now looking forward to their industrialized future instead of valuing the old.

I did not buy the collection, as I was concerned about the fragility of the pottery and the length of time before I returned to the United States. I did, however, buy a small turquoise, ninth-century oil lamp that was excavated near Gorgan on the Caspian seacoast. I had seen a similar oil lamp in the National Museum of Iran.

My Persian oil lamp

Shopping for food had never been easy in Tehran. It always seemed as if I had to go out and gather food. There were no supermarkets. If you wanted to buy meat, you had to go to a butcher shop. If you wanted fruits and vegetables, you had to visit the vegetable market. Bread was only available at the neighborhood bakery. There were also small convenience-type stores that sold canned goods and staples. We fondly called these small stores *koochies* (*koocheek* means small).

But fortunately, food and other basic necessities were reasonably priced due to government price controls and subsidies. Also, the imported food was not heavily taxed like most other imported products.

The price controls were most noticeable at the vegetable market. As you walked in, you saw only the worst quality produce displayed in the fruit and vegetable bins. This included marble-sized potatoes and onions and wilted carrots the diameter of a pencil.

This produce was being sold at very inexpensive prices as regulated by the government. However, I eventually learned that if I wanted to buy the good produce, I had to ask for it and pay a higher black-market price under the table. Even the vegetable market was not without its politics.

Gasoline was also subsidized, as it sold at an equivalent price of about twenty-five cents per gallon. This seemed like a good bargain for Americans as gasoline in the US was priced at about sixty-five cents per gallon. There were several large gasoline stations in the downtown area that sold only gasoline, diesel, kerosene, and oil. They were self-serve, but you didn't have to pay in advance, as there was always an attendant waiting nearby for you to fill your tank. You would then pay him in cash, and he would make change from a large roll of bills kept in his pocket.

Tehran was truly an international city when it came to its restaurants. One advantage I enjoyed by living downtown was that I would have my choice of eating at many of Tehran's fine international restaurants. This even included a Mexican restaurant. It wasn't the usual Tex-Mex I was familiar with, but it was quite good anyway.

My favorite restaurant was the *chelo kebab* (rice and grilled lamb) restaurant which served only two lamb kabob dishes. My neighborhood chelo kebab restaurant was a convenient walk from my apartment. It was small and brightly lit with its white, tiled walls reflecting the light from the bare florescent bulbs on the ceiling.

The chelo kebab consisted of a generous plate piled high with long-grain rice and a large, marinated lamb kebab. They also offered *koubedeh*, which was seasoned ground lamb served kebab-style on a skewer. Both always included a grilled tomato and a raw egg served over the hot steaming rice. It was then topped off with a sprinkling of sumac.

Sumac is a tangy spice made from the ground sumac berry, which grows wild in parts of the Middle East and North Africa. It has a lemony taste with the texture and color of coffee, and the Persians usually included it with rice and kebab dishes.

The only utensils available on the chrome kitchen dinette-style tables were a fork and a tablespoon without the expected knife. You were served large pieces of lamb kebab, which needed to somehow be cut into smaller pieces. I learned their technique from watching the Iranian patrons cut their kebabs. They would hold the meat in place with the fork and cut it using the edge of the tablespoon. After a little practice, I soon mastered their method of using the tablespoon as a knife.

While in season, ears of corn were roasted inside the husk over charcoal grills on the downtown sidewalks and sold to pedestrians. You always knew the location of the corn vendors by the ravens that perched in the sycamore trees above the grills. They were there patiently waiting for someone to discard a partially eaten ear of corn.

But these weren't the crows I was familiar with, although though they sounded the same. These were black-and-white pied crows that had arrived in Tehran from Africa via the pet trade. They had either escaped from captivity or were purposely released and had flourished in Tehran's urban environment. These intelligent birds had been observed using tools to forage for food and could be taught to speak a limited vocabulary in captivity. Some people claimed that these crows could even understand the meaning of some words they spoke.

As spring turned to summer, there were now demonstrations on the streets of Tehran fomenting revolution to overthrow the Shah's government. The Ayatollah Khomeini had emerged from relative obscurity in Paris and now became the spiritual leader of this movement. His defiant persona was now being used as a rallying cry to garner support for their conservative cause.

The first incident I actually witnessed happened one morning as I was crossing through the traffic on Sephabod Zahedi in the middle of the block. I was on my way to the pastry shop across the street from the office. As I was wading through the bumper-to-bumper traffic in the middle of the block, I noticed an armored army vehicle stuck in the traffic. A group of young hoodlums suddenly appeared and began attacking the soldiers with rocks and bricks while shouting their revolutionary slogans. The soldiers offered no resistance and safely retreated inside the top hatch of their vehicle.

Even though there were now antigovernment demonstrations on the streets of downtown, on Tuesday, July 4, 1978, Ben and Shirley threw a company-sponsored poolside barbeque at their villa in north Tehran for all employees and their families. We proudly flew our colors that day and celebrated our independence with country and western music, spicy Texas-style barbeque, and ice-cold Iranian barley water. Shirley was in charge of the party, as it was her traditional role as the colonel's wife. The celebration lifted everyone's spirits, and we were proud to be Americans!

Fourth of July party at Ben and Shirley's villa

I was soon to qualify for my second R&R leave, as I had been in-country for almost an entire year. I decided to take cash in lieu of a round-trip coach ticket to my home of record and instead used the money to do some traveling inside Iran. There were no travel restrictions placed on Americans, and I wasn't really too concerned about the political situation.

I talked up my travel intentions with my colleagues at work, and several indicated their willingness to also see more of Iran. Our first trip was a weekend getaway to visit the ruins of Persepolis. This was the ancient capitol of the Persian kingdom located about seventy kilometers from Shiraz in the southwestern part of Iran.

Our group of four, consisting of Joe, Robert, his wife Debra, and myself, traveled from Tehran to Shiraz on Iran Air on a Thursday evening after work and checked into our hotel. Early Friday morning we took a tourist bus to Persepolis and spent the entire day there exploring the ruins.

From left to right, Joe, Robert, Debra, and John at the Achaemenid Griffin at Persepolis

John with relief carvings at Persepolis

Persepolis was the magnificent capitol of the Archaemenid Empire. It's a complex of palaces and government buildings constructed on the terraced side of a mountain overlooking the flat plains below. It was founded by Darius in 518 BC and became the spectacular centre for the Persian kings and their empire. It was destroyed by Alexander the Great in 330 BC and has since become one of the world's greatest archaeological treasures.

On the flat plain below Persepolis, we could see the site of the Shah's celebration in October 1971 of the 2,500-year anniversary of the founding of the Persian Empire. At great expense, he built an extravagant star-shaped tented city and invited the world's leaders to attend his lavish four-day festivity. Vice President Spiro T. Agnew attended as the official representative of the United States. There were few Iranians, though, who were invited to attend the party.

While the tent city was no longer there, you could still see the star-shaped imprint left behind by the site's infrastructure and foundations of the tented structures. The Shah was criticized by his detractors for the great extravagance of his seemingly personal festivities.

Overlooking Persepolis and the star-shaped 2,500-year celebration site in the upper right-hand corner

Our group took the tourist bus back to Shiraz that evening. Sunday was spent touring the local Islamic architecture and the Tomb of Hafez, which was built to honor an ancient Persian poet who continued to be popular in modern times. Sunday evening we returned to Tehran on Iran Air as scheduled.

Visiting the Tomb of Hafez

Touring Islamic architecture in Shiraz

In conjunction with the Shah's celebration in Persepolis, the Shahyad Tower (Kings' Memorial) was dedicated in Tehran also during October 1971. It further commemorated the 2,500-year anniversary of the founding of the Persian Empire.

It's a massive memorial designed with an Islamic triumphal arch clad in white marble. This monument was the western gateway to the city, as you had to drive under it when traveling from the Mehrabad International Airport to the downtown area. I first admired this magnificent monument shortly after arriving at Mehrabad on that memorable Thursday afternoon.

The Shah was also condemned for the extravagant expense of this memorial to honor all the Persian shahs, including himself, the King of Kings. Like the Persepolis celebration, this tribute was also considered excessive by his critics.

Shahyad Tower in Tehran (1978)

The second trip our group took that summer was another weekend getaway. But this time we would be driving over the Alborz mountain range to the small Caspian seacoast village of Mahmoud. We hired Abbas as our driver for the weekend. He was the substitute driver who sometimes filled in at work and drove a four-door sedan large enough for the driver and five passengers.

With Ben's permission, the six of us left work at noon on a hot Thursday afternoon in September. We then traveled northeast out of Tehran on the winding two-lane Highway 79 past the awesome Mount Damavand.

Mount Damavand is a cone-shaped, potentially active volcano, which, at 18,406 feet, is the highest peak in Iran and the highest volcano in Asia. It holds a special place in Persian mythology and is mentioned in Persian poetry and literature. This mountain is located forty-one miles northeast of Tehran.

The road then turned north, taking us over the spectacular summit of the Alborz mountain range and down through the clouds. The climate quickly changed from hot, arid to cool, lush tropical as we drove past the rice paddies downhill to the small town of Qaemshar. We took our time and stopped along the way, taking pictures at various scenic vista points.

Our driver, Abbas, was more than just our driver. He was also our guide, our translator, and our protector when the time came. We were now headed west on Highway 22, which connected to the northern road that led to the small town of Mahmoud on the Caspian seacoast.

We approached a level stretch of the two-lane highway where the traffic had backed up and come to a stop. We thought it was possibly due to an accident, but as the traffic moved slowly forward, an army checkpoint came into view on the right side of the road. The soldiers were not stopping all vehicles, but only certain ones, and were waving the rest through. We speculated that these troops could perhaps be looking for someone or even some sort of contraband. We didn't know.

When it came our turn, we all held our breaths as the soldiers recognized us as foreigners and motioned our vehicle over for closer inspection. They first asked for our passports and then continued with all of their questioning in Farsi. While we understood the word passport, we uncomfortably could not understand the soldiers' questions. With a friendly demeanor, Abbas answered the soldiers' questions with confidence. They wanted to know who we were and why we were there. They also inquired where we were traveling from and our final destination. We all breathed a collective sigh of relief as the soldiers did not perceive us as being a threat and allowed us to go on our way.

Abbas was familiar with some beach shacks that were for rent on a daily basis just outside of Mahmoud located on the beach of the

Caspian Sea. He had stayed there before and recommended we do the same. These were sturdy, freestanding, one-room masonry buildings with steep angled roofs of corrugated tin meant to ward off the heavy rains. They all had comfortable front porches the same width as the building.

Each structure consisted of one room large enough to comfortably hold us all. However, this was just a basic roof over our heads, as there were no furnishings or indoor plumbing. Fortunately, though, it did have electrical power. The best thing about it was we only had to step outside the front door to be on the beach. We had all purchased sleeping bags in Tehran especially for this trip, in anticipation of staying in this type of rustic beach housing.

After we settled in, it seemed like a time of innocence in a faraway place where we dug our toes into the sand, enjoyed our *abjos*, and watched the sun disappear over the horizon. The revolution for us had quickly faded away just like the sunset. It was now time to build a bonfire and have a few more cold ones while passing the time away by playing spades and spinning our tales. We then turned in to snooze in our sleeping bags on the hard floor of our Spartan accommodations until morning. Our group stayed two nights at the beach shack before reluctantly returning to Tehran on Saturday afternoon.

Say cheers! On the beach at the Caspian Sea. From left to right: John, Abbas, Lee, Joe, and Debra. Robert was the photographer.

Freda had talked about the political unrest for some time now. While there were a number of reasons for the political strife, both secular and nonsecular, the two major issues had remained unchanged since the Ayatollah Khomeini first clashed with the Shah's government in the early sixties. These issues continued to concern the unequal distribution of wealth and the westernization of Iran. Both had created resentment among a growing portion of the population.

The wealth from the Shah's industrialization policies had not trickled down to everyone. It seemed to have created a mostly younger, economic underclass that was ripe for a change. These people realized there would be little prosperity available in their future under the Shah's rule. They chose to back the revolution instead of supporting a shah who had always lived in the lap of absolute luxury and power.

But the Shah traditionally lived as shahs had always lived in Persia for the past 2,500 years. Most people accepted that Shah Mohammad Reza Pahlavi would continue to live in the same opulent, autocratic way as always. He had bequeathed several titles on himself, including Imperial Majesty, which was appropriate for a shah, but he also called himself *Shahanshah* (King of Kings).

There was a vast gulf between the haves and the have-nots. You only had to walk out to the street to see it. There, you could see a *nouveau riche* man in his new Mercedes stuck in the traffic alongside a poor man riding a donkey. The irony of it was the man on the donkey could maneuver faster through the traffic than the Mercedes.

The affluent people of Tehran lived in the most desirable northern parts of the city where the altitude was higher, the temperatures were cooler, and the air was cleaner. The disadvantaged lived in the southern part of the city where just the opposite was true.

North Tehran neighborhood

The Iranians I came into contact with at work were typically educated professional people who had prospered under the Shah's regime. They were genuinely worried about the political upheaval, and none of these people wanted to see a change in the government.

The westernization of Iran that occurred under the Shah was evident as well. He had allied himself with the West and was perceived by the political right as a puppet of America and its culture. While he appeared to be rooted in Persian traditions, he seemed to be more interested in Western customs.

Many Iranian people had embraced the imported Western products, which were viewed to be superior in quality. Western automobiles were common and appeared to be a status symbol among the well-to-do. Western-styled clothing was popular as well. It was not unusual to see females in public who had now shunned wearing the traditional chador.

There was even an Iran-American Society that had established a center in north Tehran to promote cultural ties between the two countries to bring them closer together. This organization also had locations in Isfahan, Shiraz, and Mashad, as well as an office located in Washington, DC.

These cultural centers taught English to the Iranians and Farsi to the Westerners. They even offered Iranian students educational exchanges to America. They became magnets to those Iranians attracted to the liberalization influences of America.

There were, however, some elements of their culture that had remained unchanged by the unwelcome Western influence. The Persians had their own style of popular music, and they loved it. Never once did I notice American rock and roll being played in Tehran.

In addition, there were no golden arches or any other franchised American fast-food restaurants to be found in Tehran. The fast food in Tehran was typically available at sandwich shops and in pizza and Turkish kebab restaurants. Over time, I had developed an insatiable craving for an American fast-food double cheeseburger and large fries.

I now realized the importance of keeping a low profile by blending in and not being easily recognized in public as an American. Fortunately for me, I already had dark brown hair, brown eyes, and usually a tan on my face. I was also able to grow the large horseshoe-shaped moustache covering the upper lip that was popular with many Iranians.

I completed my Iranian cover with an olive drab Vietnam-era army field jacket, denim jeans, and white tennis shoes. I found that by blending in with the Iranians, I could comfortably move around the downtown area with impunity. I always made sure I looked straight ahead, never making direct eye contact or speaking with anyone on the street.

My colleagues at the office and I were now a bit uneasy as we saw certain businesses and buildings begin to burn surreptitiously under the cover of darkness. We also noticed that these arson attacks were never picked up by the BBC or reported by the English edition of the *Daily Kayhan*. This newspaper had become increasingly conservative and now openly supported the revolution.

The first burned business I noticed was a disco on Sepabod Zahedi Street near the office. The disco was located in the basement of a commercial building and had windows at the sidewalk level. When I would walk by at night, I could hear the pulsating disco beat and see the colored lights flashing through the translucent, frosted windows. It was a popular hangout with a group of young people usually waiting on the steps leading down to the double-door entrance for admission.

The disco had now been torched using *naft* as an accelerant. This was evident by the upward rising black smudges left on the outside wall from the petroleum-based smoke that leaked out around the still-intact windows. While the fire was localized in the basement and destroyed the disco, the rest of the building appeared to have survived intact.

The banks were also targeted. I noticed that the lobbies of two banks had burned in the downtown area with the same black-smoke signature of *naft*. In time, all the banks would close due to the lack of security.

The last movie I had seen while in Tehran was named in Farsi, *Jangah Saytaray. Jangah* means war, and *saytaray* means star, which in English translated as *Star Wars.* But the dialog of *Star Wars* had been dubbed in Farsi, and there were no English subtitles. While I enjoyed watching the movie with all its graphic action and strange, colorful characters, I really understood nothing of the story line.

I discovered someone had declared *jangah* on the *Star Wars* movie theater, as it now lay in a smoldering ruin. Many of the theaters across Iran would suffer a similar fate, and all would eventually be shuttered and closed.

The Buick dealership was attacked as well. Not only were the buildings torched, but all the new vehicles waiting on the lot to be sold were also destroyed by fire using *naft* as an accelerant. As part of their anti-Westernization campaign, the revolutionists had picked on the Buick dealership because it was an American company selling an American-made product. Other Western car dealerships would be destroyed in a similar fashion. Although I understood that it made a graphic political statement, it just seemed to be a total waste of new cars.

I noted that the revolutionists would burn other businesses, but I really had no way of knowing their motive. I assumed perhaps it was because the merchants were selling alcohol.

Alcohol was viewed by the conservative right as a Western evil that had been exported to Iran. It was still readily available but had visibly disappeared from the store shelves. It was now out of sight below the counter, and you knew to quietly ask for it as though you were in a speakeasy.

The Iran-American Society's Cultural Center in north Tehran would also not be forgotten. While it would survive the first round of attacks, the building in which I had taken my Farsi lessons would eventually lie in a pile of rubble. Its organization would quickly go away.

When December arrived, I noticed that Christmas trees were not being sold on the streets of downtown as before. Ben also announced there would be no company-sponsored Christmas party that year. He said our Christmas celebration had been cancelled due to circumstances far beyond a mere colonel's sphere of control.

On Tuesday, January 16, 1979, Freda informed everyone at work the Shah had fled Iran. The streets outside were soon crowded with demonstrators and cars noisily celebrating his departure. They were waving their flags and banners, shouting their slogans, and honking their obnoxious horns.

It's human nature that hope typically follows worry. I now had hope that the successor government the Shah left in place would succeed, and the strife would somehow come to a peaceful end. But deep inside, I possessed only a limited amount of optimism, and I knew this was unlikely to happen. I then went home to listen to the BBC to find out what our British friends were reporting.

The BBC confirmed what Freda had told us earlier. Without officially abdicating, the Shah and his family had departed Tehran for Cairo. The deposed Shah symbolically carried with him a small container filled with Iranian soil.

The Shah had been diagnosed with cancer five years earlier during 1974. While this was a closely held secret, it was rumored in the expatriate community that his health had recently declined. There was further speculation that although the ailing Shah still had the power to militarily bring an end to the revolution, he no longer had the personal will to do so. The Shah chose to spare his people this pain and made his decision to peacefully go into exile instead.

It was shortly after the Shah left Iran when we noticed a black, southbound Mercedes Benz 600 four-door sedan stuck in the gridlocked traffic below our offices. It was obviously transporting an important government official, as this diplomatically styled state vehicle was flying a small Iranian flag on each front fender.

As the large Mercedes slowly moved forward in traffic, we could see it was being chauffeured by an army soldier. The single passenger in the rear seat was wearing an army officer's uniform decorated with ribbons, medals, and four gold stars that shined in the sunlight. Because he was riding in one of the most prestigious government vehicles available, we speculated this general could well be the chief of staff of the Iranian army.

Almost immediately, four revolutionary hooligans appeared from nowhere and began assaulting the large sedan by rocking the car from side to side. Both the driver and the general quickly scrambled outside and abandoned the vehicle.

The driver fled for his life downhill and hastily disappeared. The general calmly walked past the rear of the vehicle and then turned around to face his adversaries. With the look of thunder on his face, he pulled out his sidearm and quickly fired off two warning shots into the air.

His attackers got the message straight away and quickly vanished onto the crowded sidewalks. The general then holstered his pistol. With an air of self-confidence, he turned his back and swaggered up the middle of the street, through the traffic, and out of sight.

Once assured that the armed four-star general had left the area and no longer posed a threat to them, the ruffians returned their attention back to the Mercedes. Everyone stuck in the nearby surrounding traffic began slowly moving their vehicles as far away from the unprotected sedan as possible. They knew what was likely to happen next.

The four men were intent on burning the car but did not possess an accelerant, as this was an unplanned, opportunistic attack. They did manage to find a cardboard box that they tore into pieces and attempted to light with matches as kindling to set fire to the interior of the car. The men were unsuccessful, as it was a windy day, and the wind blew out the matches before the cardboard ignited.

One of the men then removed the gas tank cap and proceeded to drop several lit matches, one at a time, down into the fuel intake nozzle opening. As each match dropped, I braced myself to witness a fiery explosion that would not only destroy the vehicle but perhaps its attackers as well. Nothing happened, though, and I thought it was perhaps because there was not enough oxygen in the gas tank nozzle to sustain a lit match.

I then heard gunfire from the north and saw several armed soldiers running down the middle of the street toward the Mercedes 600 and firing their AK-47 assault rifles into the air. The general had apparently notified them of the assault. The attackers scattered and quickly disappeared as before. The soldiers then took possession of the undamaged vehicle and pushed it down the street. They were unable to start it, as the driver had apparently taken the ignition keys with him when he fled south.

Our customer, Sauzi Helicopter Iran, had never mentioned canceling our contract, and Shell had never encouraged our evacuation. Construction work even continued unabated on our helicopter-manufacturing facility in Isfahan. There was still some hope the political situation would be resolved, and some semblance of normalcy would return.

Freda was street-smart and had inside information from her friends and family on the day-to-day activities of the revolutionists. She was usually able to fill us in on what was going to happen the next day. Whether it was a strike, a demonstration, a work slowdown, or a disruption of traffic, she always seemed to know what was planned. It all became an intense drama that was played out in the nearby downtown area.

In reality, though, while we understood we would probably soon be departing Iran, none of us were really in a big hurry to leave. We had all grown fairly comfortable with the Persian culture and were now making more money than we ever had before. In addition, not one of the employees in our office had ever been personally threatened by anyone.

We all attempted to keep a low profile, which only made good sense. Mostly, though, we just had to stay out of the way. If we saw an antigovernment demonstration coming down the street, we only had to walk one block over to avoid it and continue on our way. For the most part, these demonstrations were noisy and a bit rowdy but peaceful overall. But even though these were exciting, uncertain times, most of us were willing to stick it out with Shell until told otherwise.

Antigovernment demonstration in Tehran

On two different occasions, I had to quickly duck inside a storefront business because the army soldiers were clearing the sidewalks for some unknown reason. Both times the shop proprietors locked the doors and provided safe refuge for myself and others until the military action had ceased.

Revolutionary graffiti was everywhere. The demonstrators had smashed the large, plate-glass windows on many of the commercial buildings downtown. Instead of repairing the windows and risking having them broken again, the landlords and owners replaced the broken glass with semipermanent sheets of painted plywood, which then became vast billboards for graffiti.

There was graffiti near the office on a sheet of the painted plywood that got my attention. I snapped a picture of it when I thought no one was looking my way. Ever since the Picnic Day incident, I was reluctant to carry my camera in public at all. I realized that possessing a camera tended to identify you as a foreigner, which could cause you some unwanted grief.

John Robert Tipton

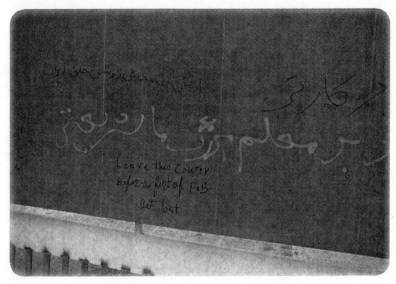

Revolutionary graffiti in downtown Tehran

We all took notice and at first assumed that because this graffiti was written in English, it was aimed at foreigners and those guilty Americans in particular. But we later realized the message could have been written earlier and directed at the Shah, even though it wasn't addressed to anyone. We tried to rationalize it away by saying it was probably just a kid practicing his English, but we had no way of knowing for sure either way.

My favorite graffiti, which seemed to be everywhere, was produced by spraying black paint on a small stencil of a stern-looking Ayatollah Khomeini. There was no text, but the message was obvious: Beware, the Ayatollah is coming, and he is unhappy!

In order to gain the public's support and approval, the new government declared a politically inspired National Open Bank Day on Monday, January 29, 1979. Effective for one day only, the participating banks would open and give their depositors the welcome opportunity to withdraw their money from previously inaccessible accounts. This was a popular move on behalf of the government that would not be opposed by the political right, as their money had been unreachable as well. The banks received the government's commitment to provide adequate beefed-up security on this date.

This was potentially good news for Shell, as the company had $253,000 frozen in our account at the Bank of Rotterdam just south of the office. I previously notified Ray Cole in Fort Worth by memo via the pouch that the banks had closed. It was doubtful we would ever be able to withdraw the money. Ray promptly answered my memo, but it struck me as being odd that he really didn't seem too concerned about this problem. But I now knew I might be able to get a cashier's check and close out the account.

I also knew that if I was successfully able to pull this off, then my picture just might make the front page of the *Shell Helicopter News*. I even fanaticized about the recognition in store for me when I returned back to Fort Worth. I knew every manager and vice president at Shell would surely remember me as the corporate hero who rescued the company's money from the clutches of the Iranian Revolution. Conceivably, I could be rewarded with a raise or maybe even longevity if I managed to keep my nose clean. Perhaps there would be yet another promotion somewhere down the road.

The political importance to my career at Shell was paramount in my mind as I decided to attempt to close our bank account. I did not inform Ben of my plans, as I had selfishly decided not to share my kudos with anyone.

I took a random vacation day off work on Monday, January 29. I got up early, as I had not slept well in anticipation of the next day's events. Before eight o'clock, I got invisibly dressed, wearing my jeans, sweatshirt, tennis shoes, and army field jacket before heading south to the bank on Ferdosi Avenue near the Grand

Tehran Bazaar. It was about a half hour walk downhill to the Bank of Rotterdam, but it was quite cold and windy that day.

With my field jacket collar held against my neck to ward off the cold, I continued downhill on Sephabod Zahedi. Snow flurries began to fall as I crossed Takht-e-Jamshid (Throne of Jamshid) Avenue. This street was the main commercial east-west corridor in downtown. I noticed this was the first snowfall for the winter and hoped for no accumulation on my apartment building's roof.

The American embassy compound, which occupied a large city block of twenty-six acres, was located just a few blocks to the east on Takhte-e-Jamshid Avenue. It was an unimposing, two-story red-brick building with a long, low profile that made it resemble an older American high school.

Upon crossing Takht-e-Jamshid and passing by Maydoneh Ferdosi (Ferdosi Traffic Circle), the name of the street changed from Sephabod Zahedi to Ferdosi Avenue. This street led to the Tehran Bazaar. It was well known for its large number of Persian carpet dealers and antique shops that soon came into view on both sides of the street. Most of these businesses had now closed their doors to wait out the political strife.

Upon first arriving in Tehran, one of my initial tasks was to open a bank account for the company. The Bank of Rotterdam came highly recommended to Ben, and I was directed to open our company account there. Foreign banks were allowed to operate in Iran, but all were required to be in partnership with an established Iranian bank. In this case, the Bank of Rotterdam was partnered with the prestigious Bank Meli, which was the central bank of Iran and the custodian of the Persian crown jewels.

The Imperial Crown Jewels of Persia is the world's largest collection of jewelry. It was collected by the Iranian Monarchy over a period of 2,500 years and was now considered so valuable that it was used to back the Iranian currency. It was safeguarded by Bank Meli with many of the major pieces of the collection on public display in the Jewelry Museum. This museum was located in a large vault in the basement of the Bank Meli building in downtown Tehran.

I visited the Jewelry Museum on a Saturday afternoon, which was my Sunday, as it was the last day of the weekend. The museum was located within walking distance of my apartment. There was a small admission fee and prominent signage written in several different languages at the entrance to the large vault warning: "DO NOT TOUCH THE GLASS DISPLAY CASES. IF YOU DO, AN ALARM WILL SOUND, AND SECURITY WILL RESPOND!"

I entered the museum and could see a large number of glass cases randomly placed throughout the vault displaying a dazzling array of jewel-encrusted objects. The glass cases were almost seamless, allowing an unobstructed view of the display. You were able to completely walk around most cases, which allowed visitors a 360-degree view of some jeweled items.

With my eyes opened wide, I examined the unbelievable collection of jeweled crowns, thrones, tiaras, necklaces, bracelets, huge loose stones, and so many other pieces. I was just admiring the incredibly jeweled Imperial Globe of Persia with its fifty-one thousand precious stones when I heard the loud pulsating alarm sound. At the same time, the massive double vault doors immediately slammed shut. Someone had touched one of the glass display cases!

Five deadly serious security guards immediately appeared from nowhere. The one in charge then vociferously ordered in both Farsi and English, "*Everyone freeze! Do not move!*"

All the museum visitors complied and froze in place as ordered. I could see these security guards were not the usual guards you would expect to see at a museum. They were not uniformed with badges or insignia, but instead were in plain clothes, wearing Western-styled suits with coats and ties. They reminded me of the somber-looking US Secret Service agents you would see guarding the president. I noticed the subtle outline of sidearms under their coats, but no one pulled a gun. The alarm was then silenced, and the guards completed their visual inspection of the glass cases and the visitors. Because they could find nothing amiss, the vault doors were then opened, and everyone was allowed to continue with their visit as before.

I hurriedly walked a couple more blocks and could now see the Bank of Rotterdam in the distance on the left side of the street. It was now only about eight-thirty and the bank would not open until nine o'clock, but the crowd of customers waiting to withdraw their money stretched around the block. An army vehicle with several soldiers armed with standard issue AK-47 rifles was stationed near the entrance to ensure the bank's security. I soon joined this line as I patiently waited with the rest of the bank's depositors to withdraw their money.

The manager of the Bank of Rotterdam was Theo Van Der Veer, a tall, friendly Dutchman who always gave you a firm handshake and a welcoming smile. I always enjoyed conversing with Theo about the revolution, which was constantly rife with rumors. He always had some good ones, which I would promptly take back to the office and spread around.

My signature was the only one required on the signature authorization card. I was authorized to write checks with no upward limits on the amount. I always deposited dollar checks into the account, which were then converted into riyals at the official prevailing rate for that day.

The bank opened its doors promptly at nine, and the line in front of me slowly dwindled. By eleven o'clock I had just made it inside the front door when I saw Theo stepping out of his office with some papers in hand. As he walked out into the crowded lobby, I waved and shouted out his name, "Hey, Theo. *Theo*!"

He then looked up, saw me standing in the line, and nodded his recognition. Upon completion of his task, he went to his office door, opened it, and motioned for me to leave the line and to step into his office.

There wasn't much time this day for the usual small talk, and it was obvious why I was there.

I smiled as I said, "Theo, I'll bet you already know why I'm here this morning."

He replied, "Yes I do, John. You and half of Tehran are here. Fortunately, the government treasury ministry has been busy printing riyals overtime, and I think we have enough money on hand to pay everyone."

I was pleased to hear that good news as I replied, "Well, that sounds great. You know I'm here to close out our account. What I need is a dollar cashier's check to be made out to the Shell Helicopter Company for our remaining balance of $253,000 and change."

With a concerned look, Theo answered, "I can get you a cashier's check, but the Iranian branch of the Bank of Rotterdam is closing its doors permanently tomorrow. The check would never clear the bank upon being deposited. I do not have dollars, but I can pay you the $253,000 in Iranian riyals."

I had learned to expect the unexpected during difficult times, but I never anticipated this.

I then nodded my head affirmatively as I said, "Thanks, Theo. Riyals will work just fine."

Theo then left his office and returned shortly with a check made out to Shell Helicopter in the amount of 936,100 riyals. This amount was based on the current exchange rate for that day of 3.70 riyals to the dollar. I then endorsed the back of the check and patiently waited while Theo went personally to the vault to retrieve the money and close out the account.

It seemed to take forever, but he finally returned pushing a cart piled high with paper-banded bundles of newly printed one-hundred-riyal notes. Each bundle held one hundred bills, which totaled ten thousand riyals and bore the official certification stamp of the Iranian Ministry of the Treasury. There were ninety-three complete bundles and one partial that held the remaining 6,100 riyals. Theo then handed me a photocopy of the check along with the account closure documents, which I immediately signed.

This was a big pile of cash that was totally unforeseen. I didn't know what I could possibly do with all of this money. I came to the bank anticipating only a check, but now I had all of these bundles of riyals to deal with. I needed some sort of bag in which to put the money. I knew the best place in this neighborhood to find something like that was the nearby Grand Tehran Bazaar.

The Tehran Bazaar was well known for its conservative zeal, as it had provided political and financial support for the revolution. The merchants, a traditional class known as *bazaaris*, feared losing their status and political power as they were left behind by the Shah's industrialization of the country.

I had visited the bazaar before but always during more peaceful times. Because it was now known as a hotbed of revolutionary activity, I had chosen to avoid it as part of my ongoing effort to maintain my low profile.

I then departed the bank into the cold, blowing wind, turned left on Ferdosi, and headed south toward the bazaar. After a few blocks, the street curved to the west, and the northern main entrance of the sprawling ancient brick bazaar came into view on the left side of the street.

I then entered and could now see the copper handicrafts, the Persian carpet shops, the gold dealers, and the antique shops clustered around the main entrance specifically for the tourist trade. During my previous visits, the bazaar had always bustled with customers, but not today. The revolution had definitely taken its toll on these shopkeepers' business.

Copper handicrafts at the bazaar.

I continued to head south in the arched main corridor, always farther downhill into the bowels of the dimly lit ancient labyrinth where Tehran residents could do their everyday shopping. I then walked through the food areas past the pungent smells of the spice dealers and the inviting small kebab restaurants.

I then turned left and entered an adjoining corridor I always thought of as the plastic bazaar. These shops were completely filled from floor to ceiling with every plastic product imaginable.

I soon spotted a small shop displaying a variety of suitcases. I noticed a small, zippered vinyl one hanging on the wall that I felt would securely hold all the money. There were others to choose from, but I preferred this particular one because it was green, the color of a four-leaf clover and the color of my good luck. I was confident this color would help give the valise a special ability to protect its contents from harm.

I then removed it from the wall and silently handed it to the shopkeeper. I said nothing as I had no desire to divulge my nationality in one of the most conservative places in all of Iran. I then handed the proprietor, in exact change, the marked asking price of sixty-five riyals. This was unusual, as it was customary to negotiate for a lower price for anything you bought in the bazaar.

I believe my failure to bargain helped reveal my nationality as the proprietor made eye contact and curtly asked in English, "You're an American, aren't you?"

I was totally taken aback but managed to answer with an air of self-assurance in my best Farsi, "*Bally ahgah, Americayee hastam. Irannee nistam.*" (Yes, mister, I am an American. I am not Iranian.)

He replied, "The streets outside can be dangerous for Americans. Be safe, be well, my friend."

I had fully anticipated a confrontation with this man. Now, in the deepest, darkest part of the wolf's lair, I had just been treated with respect and kindness.

I breathed a sigh of relief as I politely thanked him by saying, *"Merci ahgah, kaylee motshakaram."* (Thanks, mister. Thank you very much.) I then nodded farewell as I added, *"Khoda hafez eh shomah."* (Good-bye to you.)

I turned around carrying my new suitcase and retraced my path back to the main corridor. I then turned right and headed uphill toward the northern entrance, thankful my final visit to the bazaar was totally uneventful.

I arrived at the bank and passed quickly through the crowded lobby to Theo's office. I knocked on the locked door, identified myself, and quickly gained entrance. The money was just as I had left it, piled high on a cart in the middle of the room. I then began transferring the money from the cart to the suitcase and counting it at the same time. It was all there, and the small suitcase was stuffed full but was just large enough to hold it all.

I then turned to Theo and said, "Okay, Theo, my friend. Thanks for everything, and I hope you and your family have safe passage out of Iran."

He replied, "And the same to you, John. When the air traffic resumes, we hope to be on the first KLM flight to Schiphol."

He then escorted me out a side door, and I turned north onto the crowded Ferdosi Avenue toward home. It was chilly as the snow continued to fall and began to noticeably drift against the curbs and buildings.

I had walked only a couple of blocks when I realized my suitcase was getting increasingly heavy with every step taken. The events of the day had taken their toll, and the accompanying adrenaline rush had now ceased to flow. I knew then I wanted to walk no farther uphill and would have to take one of the shared orange taxis that filled the main streets of downtown Tehran.

In order to get one of these taxis to stop, you had to stand on the curb and shout out your destination as the taxi passed by. In this case, I had to continuously shout out the street name Abassabad, which was the main boulevard just north of my small residential street. After being seemingly ignored by a number of taxis, I was relieved when one finally stopped for me and my precious cargo.

After the taxi pulled over to the curb and stopped, the driver got out and opened the trunk to put my bag inside. There was no room in the taxi for it, as there were already three passengers. He then placed the suitcase on top of the other passenger's belongings and gently tried to squeeze the lid shut. But the small trunk was overloaded, which prevented the lid from completely closing. The driver had obviously faced this problem before, as his immediate solution was to secure the trunk lid with an old, frayed bungee cord. I then paid him the fare of three riyals for me and one for my suitcase.

As I was the fourth passenger, I had to squeeze into the most undesirable seat between the two other passengers in the middle rear seat. I was careful not to speak nor make eye contact with them as I tried to blend in by presenting myself as just another Tehran resident on my way home from work. With the taxi filled completely to capacity, we then inched slowly northward in the traffic with my quarter-million dollars hanging precariously out of the rear end secured only by a worn bungee cord.

As we approached my street, I politely asked the driver in Farsi to pull over and stop. Upon exiting the taxi, the driver released the bungee cord that secured the trunk lid and handed me my suitcase. I thanked him with a courteous merci and gave him two riyals for a tip, although it was not customary to tip the orange taxi drivers.

I then briskly walked the two blocks to my apartment building and was relieved to enter the safety of my building's locked foyer. I quickly climbed the two flights of stairs, unlocked my front door, and entered my unfurnished no room. I then crossed through to the living room and relaxed on the couch with the money by my side. I was finally able to unwind and closed my eyes as I wondered what to do with all of this cold, hard cash.

Even when the flights resumed, how could I possibly get this amount of money past Iranian customs and out of the country? At the airport they would always open and search your luggage and then pat you down prior to leaving. I also knew they had strict currency restriction laws in place. Perhaps they would arrest me for attempting to smuggle riyals out of the country. I just didn't know.

I soon became aware of the chilling cold of my unheated apartment. Iran was one of the world's largest oil producers, but because the oil workers were now on strike in support of the revolution, naft was in short supply. My landlord had previously advised that he was able to obtain only enough fuel for two weeks of heat or four weeks of hot water. At the time, I had voted for the hot water but was now having second thoughts about it.

But I hadn't eaten for the day, and I knew there was not much more than a few condiments in my refrigerator. I decided to go down to visit the neighborhood Turkish kebab restaurant. Turkish kebab, also known as *shawarma* in some places, is typically lamb or chicken meat stacked vertically on a spit and then roasted as the spit rotates. Meat shavings are then cut off the rotating spit and served in a wrap similar to a soft tortilla. The Iranians called this Turkish kebab, as it had its origins in Turkey. It was my favorite fast food in Tehran.

Upon returning from the Turkish kebab restaurant, reality set in as I opened my front door, flipped on the light switch, and was irritated that nothing happened. Not only was my apartment cold, but it was now dark and cold. But this was not the first time this had happened. In fact, it had happened so many times that electrical interruptions were now expected on a daily basis. At work, we had ceased to use the elevators, as we feared getting stuck between floors during an outage. I had bought an entire box of white dripless candles to provide light at home during the power interruptions.

The electrical unions, in sympathy with the revolution, were now on a slowdown strike, causing the shortage. In addition, with the oil workers on strike, I suspected the shortage was also due to a lack of available energy to power the grid. With no heat or electricity, the only thing left to do was to conceal the suitcase under my bed and to try to get some sleep.

My head had hardly hit the pillow when I heard a loud knock at my front door. I quickly sat up in bed as I thought to myself, *Who can possibly be knocking on my door at this time of night, and how did they get past the locked door of the foyer?*

I found it hard to believe anyone would be knocking on my door at all. I then heard the knock again, and this time it was even louder.

My thoughts began to race as my gut tightened with the dread of impending danger. It could only be my landlord or perhaps my new neighbor on the second floor. But my landlord was an older gentleman who would never be knocking on my door at this hour unless there was an emergency. In addition, I doubted it would be my new neighbor on the second floor, as we had never met. Our paths had crossed a couple of times on the stairway, and we had developed a sort of nodding acquaintance but nothing more than that. I then heard the loud knock a third time.

This time I jumped out of bed, threw on my pants, and quickly crossed from the bedroom through the no room to the front door. As I passed through the no room, I caught a glimpse through my front window of an armed army jeep double-parked on the street below.

My front door was designed with a decorative wrought-iron frame that held a large piece of patterned, translucent, rose-colored glass the same size as the door itself. As I approached the door, I could just make out several shadowy forms behind the glass. They then knocked a fourth time, and this time it was so hard the glass itself shattered and spilled across the entire no room.

On the dimly lit stairway landing, I could now see three men wearing army uniforms and black ski masks. One was definitely in charge, as I could see he was wearing the bars of a first lieutenant. He was also holding in both hands a cocked .38-caliber Smith & Wesson stainless revolver that was pointed through the wrought-iron door frame and aimed directly at my head.

In perfect English he demanded, "Unlock the door! Open this door *now!*"

I was familiar with the legendary .38-caliber police special revolver and was well aware of the damage it could inflict. There is no safety on this gun, and it only has to be cocked to be ready to fire. I knew I was not in any position to do anything other than comply with his demand. I unlocked the door, and the three men quickly entered the no room.

With the gun still aimed at me, I could see the fire in his dark eyes as he said only one thing, "Where's the money?"

I paused slightly but in shock raised my arm and pointed toward my open bedroom doorway and replied, "It's in there. The money is in the bedroom."

As the officer continued to hold the gun on me, the other two quickly entered my bedroom, and I could now hear them ransacking the room. They started with the closet and then moved to my dresser.

I knew they had found my suitcase hidden away under my bed when I heard them rapidly unzip it and excitedly exclaim something in Farsi that I could not understand. The two then returned to the no room and proudly displayed the open suitcase full of wrapped bundles of one-hundred-riyal notes to their leader.

The lieutenant said nothing but smiled as he picked up one bundle and began closely examining it. He intently stared at the money as he slowly fanned the notes with his thumb several times. He then briefly raised the bundle to his nose and smelled the subtle odor of the newly printed riyals before returning his attention back to me.

The officer then began rapidly issuing orders to his men in Farsi. I could not understand his words, but I knew what he was saying as his men grabbed my arms, twisted them behind me, and forced me to my knees. They then bent me over execution style to where my head was tucked between my legs. I could now feel the cold, hard steel of the revolver's muzzle pressed firmly against the back of my head. I was terrified!

In shocked disbelief, I understood so well what was happening and knew I could do absolutely nothing about it but beg for their mercy. With tears now welling up in my eyes, I begged for my life as I cried out, "No, no, no, you don't have to do this! You have the money. Why take my life? I can't identify you! You rotten bastards!"

But my pleas fell on their deaf ears, and I suddenly heard a sharp explosion as he pulled the trigger!

In a cold, wet sweat, I bolted upright in my bed and awakened wide-eyed from my nightmare. I looked under my bed to make sure my suitcase was still there and checked out the front door to reassure myself that the glass was not actually smashed. I was so relieved it was only a dream, as it had all seemed far too real.

The next morning I got up early, as I had not slept well, and I left for work at the normal time. When I went downstairs and stepped into my building's glassed foyer, I paused as usual, looking up and down the street for a possible unforeseen danger.

On the second of January, I taped a cardboard sign on the inside of my jeep's windshield, stating in the Farsi alphabet, *barayeah faroush* (for sale), and followed underneath by my telephone number. Freda had written the sign for me in Farsi.

I had stopped driving my jeep, as gasoline was becoming difficult to buy. The filling stations would soon close due to the oil workers strike. Gasoline would then be available only on the black market at exorbitant prices.

I had left my jeep parked on the street just outside my apartment building for more than a week now. With the uncertainty of the revolution, I had finally decided to sell it before it was too late.

As I walked past the vehicle the next morning, I noticed a small piece of folded paper under the windshield wiper. I opened the paper and could see someone had laboriously printed in capital block letters a note written in English stating: "YOU HAVE THIRTY DAYS TO LEAVE IRAN."

I then checked my calendar, and I could see the thirtieth day would fall on February 1. I knew I would have to take the note seriously and reported the incident to Ben the first thing that morning.

"Hey, Ben, take a look at this!" I said. "Somebody left this note on my jeep's windshield last night, and they've given me thirty days to leave the country."

Ben then took the note, read it out loud a couple of times in amazement, and chuckled. "This is really an incredible note. Someone has actually given you thirty days to get out of the country. I tend to think this is just an idle threat, but we can't take any chances. It's probably best for you to check into a hotel sometime prior to the expiration of the thirty-day deadline. I'll sign off on your hotel stay, and the company will foot the bill."

I felt better about the whole thing after speaking with Ben. At least we now had a plan, and in addition, Shell would pay my impending hotel bill.

The following morning as I left for work, I found another note under the same windshield wiper with only the number twenty-nine written on it in the same block style. Each successive morning after that, I found the same note with only the next descending number written on it in the same handwriting. The author obviously wanted to intimidate me by dramatically counting down the thirty-day deadline day by day.

On the tenth of January, I finally sold my jeep, and the notes stopped. Until then, I had only gotten a couple of inquiries over the phone concerning my asking price for the vehicle. I knew because of the revolution there would probably be few people interested in buying an old jeep. But on that day I received an offer for almost half of my asking price, and I readily accepted it. I just wanted to get rid of those damn notes!

The notes ceased after I sold the vehicle, but they continued to be responsible for the worrisome questions going through my mind. I worried about whether the notes were really serious or nothing more than a bad joke. Now, since they had gone away, had the threat itself gone away as well? I couldn't answer that one either.

I felt that the perpetrator knew where I lived, although there were no notes left on my building's front door. In addition, he must have known my telephone number, but I did not receive any threatening phone calls.

It finally occurred to me that the author of the notes could well have been the person who bought my jeep. I surmised that he cleverly wrote the notes to intimidate me into selling the jeep at a rock-bottom price. Even though I came to the logical conclusion I had been scammed, I still cautiously continued to check out the street every time I left my building.

I walked to work that morning as usual, dodging the mopeds that had taken to the sidewalks to avoid the traffic-choked streets. I had also grown accustomed to watching for—and stepping over—the uncovered jubes that lined the streets. If you accidentally stepped into one of these things, you could easily be injured.

The jubes were uncovered gutters between the sidewalk and the street that were flushed with water twice a day. The water was released each morning and afternoon from a mountain reservoir high above the city. Because the system was gravity fed and Tehran was on the downward slope, adequate pressure was never a problem.

The water would start out sparkling clean in northern Tehran, but by the time it reached the southern parts of the city it would be a muddy-brown color. I observed that some people disrespected the system by discarding unwanted trash into the jubes, knowing it would soon be flushed away. It was not unusual for the jubes to become blocked with debris as the water flowed under the intersections, which sometimes resulting in minor flooding. The street workers would then dislodge the obstruction with long wooden poles. The jube water also provided irrigation for the large sycamore trees that lined most streets of downtown. The sycamores provided welcome shade for the sidewalks and offered the sound of rustling leaves when the wind blew through them.

It was rumored that the street vendors sometimes used the jube water to wash their fruits and vegetables. I had personally never seen this, but our company advised us against buying fruits and vegetables on the street. Most fruits and vegetables could be disinfected with the exception of the *toot* (strawberry), which could not be treated because of its porous skin. If you ate untreated produce, it came with the unfortunate risk that could result in a visit to the doctor.

The drinking-water supply for Tehran was potable directly from the tap and also had a pleasant taste. Every flat-roofed building in Tehran had its own water tank on the roof, which always provided adequate gravity-fed pressure for the building. The water supply flowed down from the mountains to the north and always provided adequate water for the entire city.

I arrived at work about a half hour early, as usual, and my colleagues and I gathered around Ben's shortwave radio to listen to the static-filled hourly BBC newscast from London. Promptly at eight o'clock we all heard the familiar trademark chimes of the BBC and listened carefully.

The BBC was reporting in their lead story that the Ayatollah's return from Paris to Tehran was imminent. His return was currently being negotiated with the new Iranian government. Everyone knew this meant all hell could soon break loose.

I then glanced out the second-story window and could see an eight-story building in the southern part of the city just beginning to go up in flames. This was unusual, because the building appeared to be just an average office building instead of the usual ideological targets that the opposition favored. But they had long ago exhausted these targets as they burned the discos, the car dealerships, the theaters, and anything else they considered to represent Western decadence.

Now that the Ayatollah was soon to be on his way, the emboldened revolutionaries appeared to have selected the more-substantial targets. We speculated that this burning building could possibly house an Iranian government ministry.

But I now had some work to do, and I was glad it would take my mind off what was happening outside. General Ghorbani had requested some cost data for the amount of expenses incurred to date for their helicopter factory being constructed in Esfahan. I suspected that they wanted to know the extent of their termination liability in case the contract was cancelled. I didn't have all the information together, but I had some preliminary numbers I could give him with the promise of better updated information to follow.

I finished putting my numbers together and walked up the stairway to the fourth floor to deliver my interim estimate to General Ghorbani. His secretary had a small office that opened into the hallway before connecting to his office in the rear. I thought it was unusual when I saw her door was closed, and there was no answer when I gently knocked. I then attempted to turn the doorknob and, to my surprise, found that it was locked. I quickly turned around and was perplexed to see all the doors to the other generals' offices were closed as well. In fact, the entire floor was vacant.

I then ran upstairs to the fifth floor where the commanding general's managing director's office was located. I knew this was an inner sanctum of the Iranian air force, and I should not be there without a valid reason. I just had to see for myself if anyone was there.

As I stepped onto the fifth-floor landing, I could now see all the way down the length of the marbled hallway. The usually open mahogany doors were all closed, and the entire fifth floor appeared to be vacant, just as I had suspected.

I remembered having seen several of the Iranian air force civilian employees arrive and walk up the stairs just as I had arrived at work this morning. I knew this day was not some obscure Iranian holiday, and their offices should be open. But I also realized with almost certainty that the Iranian generals had some inside information we were not privy to. They had probably fled the building for their own safety. Perhaps they had listened to the same BBC newscast we had heard. In any event, I couldn't help but be a little angry they had hastily left the building without advising us to do the same.

I then ran down to the second floor and advised Ben of what I had seen on the top two floors as I excitedly exclaimed, "Ben, they've split. They're all gone!"

Ben asked, "What are you talking about? Who's all gone?"

"The generals and their staff have fled the building without saying one word to us," I answered. "We have to get out of here too!"

He then expressed his concerns as we hastily walked around each side of our floor and counted the downtown burning buildings. We could now see a total of nine buildings in flames. Most of the engulfed buildings were off in the distance, but the newly burning ones seemed to be moving in our direction. I could see the worried look on the colonel's face as the wheels continued to turn.

Ben then rapidly ordered, "Go down to the basement and get the drivers and their vehicles ready to go. I'll notify all the employees to meet in the basement so we can get the vehicles loaded and transport everyone home from there."

I momentarily imagined that I was now truly serving in Colonel Halley's militia as we hastily made our retreat from the failing front line that was soon to be breached. I quickly replied with a sharp, "Yes, sir!"

I then obeyed the colonel's order like a good trooper. I ran down to the basement to get our drivers and their vehicles cranked up and ready to go.

The problem we faced was that there was not enough room in the three Paykons to transport all of the employees at the same time. There were fifteen employees in the building who needed transportation, but there was room in the vehicles for only the drivers and twelve passengers.

To solve the problem, Ben then directed, "Okay, everybody, listen up. The employees living the farthest from the office will be taken home first. Then one vehicle will return to the office to pick up the remaining three employees and take them home."

I didn't agree with Ben's decision, but I bit my lip and said nothing. I knew his judgment meant that he would be in the first group to go, and I would be among the last three left behind. I felt that it would be best if the employees living closest to the office should be taken home first. Then one driver could quickly come back and pick up the last three. But this would mean Ben would have to stay behind instead of me. This seemed logical enough, though; as I had learned from the movies, it's the captain's duty to stay with his ship and weather the storm!

The first group of employees then left the building for home, leaving Freda, myself, and Bill Jones behind. We gathered in my corner office and watched as the burning buildings edged ever closer. We feared our building was an obvious target because of the large medallion just above the front door with The Iranian Helicopter Industry written on it in both Farsi and English.

Bill was an older guy who had worked for Shell for many years and was now looking forward to retirement after this assignment as the engineering manager. His office was next to mine, and over the past year, we had become a couple of unarmed brothers-in-arms as we both watched the revolution unfold in the streets below.

Before he left, Ben confided in me that he had been in touch with an old air force associate now assigned to the embassy. He said there was a possibility that all Shell employees could soon be evacuated from Tehran by the US Air Force. Ben added that he should definitely know about the evacuation flight by tomorrow. He would then be able to announce this good news to everyone. All of a sudden my spirits were lifted a bit, and I felt a little better about being left behind.

I considered walking home that afternoon, but I knew that the streets were entirely too dangerous for that. In addition, I didn't want to leave Freda and Bill alone in the office by themselves. I decided instead to wait for one of the drivers to return to the office and give us a ride home. Depending on the traffic, I knew that it should not take much more than an hour for the driver to return.

By midafternoon, the overdue contract driver hadn't returned to pick us up. We speculated that he couldn't make it either because the streets were blocked with burning tires, or perhaps he was just too afraid to return downtown. There was no way for us to know for sure what had really happened.

I ran downstairs to the lobby to see if the two Iranian air force military policemen manning the front desk had heard from our driver. I was astonished to find that both guards had fled their posts and were nowhere to be found. I then noticed that they had locked the double-glass front doors and also the outside accordion security grille as they departed. I ran down to the basement and found they had also secured that outside door. The guards obviously didn't know that there was anyone left inside the building. As there were no windows on the first floor that could be opened, we were now trapped and couldn't leave even if we had wanted to.

From my second-story office window, we saw a growing crowd of mostly younger men gathered on the sidewalk in the front of our building with their attention focused on our front doors and the lobby. There were no slogans or clenched fists this time. The revolutionists were now so emboldened they didn't even bother to cover their faces.

We peeked through the closed miniblinds and quietly cracked open the front window in my office so we could hear their conversation just below us. A group of them were now sitting on the stairway to nowhere directly below my office window, plotting the incendiary destruction of our building.

I then whispered to Freda, "Can you hear what they're saying? What they are planning to do?"

She replied quietly to both Bill and me, "They intend to pry off the locked accordion security grille and then smash the glass front doors to gain entrance. They will then stack all the wooden lobby furnishings at the stairwell entrance and soak them with *naft*."

Freda then paused to listen to some more of their conversation before saying, "Actually, first they plan to set a fire with *naft* on an upper-level floor before returning to the lobby and igniting the furniture. They anticipate that the fire in the lobby will burn up the stairwell and connect with the upper blaze to destroy the building."

"They have a problem, though. They have run out of *naft* and have sent two of their compatriots with money to buy some more of it on the black market."

The revolutionaries had few explosives and guns, making *naft* their weapon of necessity. The gasoline stations in Tehran had been closed ever since the oil workers' strike. Now gasoline and naft were only available on the black market at very expensive prices.

Today, there was no visible security on the streets of downtown Tehran. Usually there would be an armored army vehicle every few blocks manned by several soldiers. But it was clear that they really didn't have their hearts into it, as it was not unusual to see a soldier with a flower symbolically sticking out of the muzzle of his gun. But the caretaker government had apparently ordered the army to stay in their barracks today, allowing the revolutionaries to be unopposed. It was as if the authorities had purposely looked the other way in an effort to somehow appease the opposition.

Until now, the demonstrators were allowed to have their way in the streets of downtown and to burn their ideological targets unopposed. But today it was different. It appeared that these men were not the usual noisy demonstrators but instead an organized group of serious revolutionaries intent on doing as much damage as possible to their government.

In about a half hour, the two men returned to the front of our building carrying one twenty-liter red plastic container filled with *naft*. Their anticipated arrival excited the crowd, and they now quickly pried off the security grille with a crow bar. They then began to assault our glass doors with rocks and bricks they had collected earlier. The thick tempered glass withstood their initial attack but then fell victim to a large cinder block lobbed at it by two of the men. We heard the door smash and saw the glass spill onto the sidewalk as the mob rushed into our building.

We had already decided that if this happened we would then take refuge in the small photocopy room on the north side of the second floor. We doubted this would be an important room to our attackers, as they could easily identify it by the sign on the door, which was written in both English and Farsi. In addition, this door could be locked from the inside, and we could also use the photocopy machine to help block the door if needed. More importantly, there was a sliding-glass window in this room intended for ventilation, which could be opened.

As the front doors were smashed, Bill and I headed to the photocopy room while Freda ran to her desk to pick up her chador. After she joined us, we locked the door and quietly pushed the photocopy machine tightly against it.

Freda then whispered, "Listen!"

Almost immediately we heard a commotion in the lobby and footsteps on the stairway.

I could hear the sound of fear in her voice as Freda gasped and then whispered, "Oh no, they're coming!"

"Okay, let's put all our weight against the photocopy machine in case they try to open the door," I directed.

We then heard the intruders running through our second-floor offices and held our breaths as one of them attempted to turn the locked doorknob and open our door. We all quietly pushed against the photocopy machine with all our strength.

But just as we had hoped, they were in a hurry and apparently saw the photocopy room as being of little consequence. We then listened as the footsteps grew fainter when they left the second floor to search for a target somewhere upstairs.

Bill said in a panicked voice, "Now they're going upstairs to set a fire. We've got to get out of here!"

In a few moments we heard their footsteps rapidly descend the stairway followed by a muffled explosion from above. Shortly afterwards, we then heard and felt a louder explosion from the downstairs lobby.

Still whispering, I said, "They have to be gone. Let's open the door and take a look."

We then moved the photocopy machine aside, cracked opened the door, and could now see and smell the acrid black smoke boiling up the stairwell from the lobby below. We shut the door immediately!

Bill was visibly shaken. "Oh dear God, we've got to get out of here," he exclaimed. "How about the window? Let's check out the window!"

As smoke filled our floor, we now clearly realized we were trapped between the burning lobby below and another fire somewhere above. We also knew that the only possible route of escape was through the second-story window in the photocopy room.

We all went over to the window to investigate it as our potential escape route. As we stuck our heads outside the window, I continued to whisper as I said, "Look, I think we can climb down there."

We had seen a narrow decorative ledge running the length of the building several feet below the window. Below that was a stucco wall that was originally built for the aging villa next door. Fortunately, next to the window was a steel galvanized drainage pipe that extended down from the flat roof of the building to the ground.

At an earlier time before the Shah's industrialization, downtown Tehran had a number of large, walled villas with spacious landscaped gardens. With the economic expansion, most of these old houses had long since been torn down and replaced with new commercial buildings.

However, there was one that survived on the north side of our office building at the end of the block. It had two stories with a flat roof and a stucco wall that went completely around the outside perimeter of its lot. It was an aging house whose grandeur had long since passed. When our building was constructed next door, it was built almost touching the villa's wall, which was left undisturbed.

As we planned our escape and looked out the photocopy room window, we surveyed the villa, its grounds, and its wall just below the window. We felt that we could first lower ourselves down to the ledge and then use the drain pipe to the right of the window to continue down to the top of the wall. From there, it would be an easy matter to jump down into the villa's courtyard below.

I volunteered to go first and slowly lowered myself backward out the window down to the ledge while hanging on to the windowsill. I then grasped the drain pipe in my right hand and held on to the ledge with my left as I lowered myself down to the top of the wall. I then waited there as Freda came down next and was followed by Bill. We then safely jumped one by one down into the courtyard.

After a brief conversation concerning our next move, Freda agreed to approach the occupants of the villa and ask for temporary refuge. She then put on her chador and confidently knocked on their front door.

A male occupant opened the door, and we could see his wife with two young children gathered just behind him. They were startled that we had entered their walled compound and wanted to know why we were there. Freda explained that we had just escaped from the burning office building next door and asked for temporary shelter in their villa. They seemed to be sympathetic to our plight until Freda revealed that Bill and I were Americans. The couple then informed us that it was too dangerous for them to harbor Americans in their house, and all three of us had to leave. We were then escorted to their front gate, which opened onto the street.

Just as the steel gate was unlocked and opened, we heard several random shots ring out from down the street. To our horror, we saw Freda collapse to the sidewalk in a blackened heap.

We raised her up and could now see a neat, small-caliber wound in the upper middle of her forehead. When we looked further, we could see the exit was not so kind. We then vainly searched for a pulse and peered into her still opened eyes. Our dear Freda, our dear beloved Freda, was dead.

Bill and I were in a state of total shock and disbelief when the husband informed us we had brought enough trouble to his family. For their safety, we were asked to leave immediately. He stated he would call an ambulance for Freda and notify the authorities.

I had heard what he said, but he sounded very distant until his wife became hysterical and started screaming things that we couldn't understand. Bill and I looked at each other and knew it was time to go. We briefly knelt at Freda's side with our heads bowed while silently saying a prayer and followed with our tearful good-byes.

We exited through the gate and ran south toward the American embassy, which was several blocks away. When we reached the embassy guard shack at the rear motor-pool entrance, the marine guard crisply saluted us and quickly opened the gate.

The marine guard on duty that afternoon was my first cousin's eldest son from a small town on the high plains of eastern Colorado. Upon graduating from high school, he had secretly joined the marines without informing his parents in order to escape the boredom of a small farming town. The Marine Corps sent him to San Diego for basic training and then to Tehran as an embassy guard.

We had been to the embassy many times before to eat lunch at the cafeteria. Any American citizen was welcome to eat at their dining facility. You only had to present your passport at the gate in order to gain entry. My cousin normally worked at the rear entrance and always greeted us with a salute, usually without even the formality of checking our passports.

The American food at the embassy was good and reasonably priced, but it seemed to be the little things that made a difference. They had the round toothpicks instead of the flat ones, crystalline salt instead of sea salt, and real mayonnaise. But most importantly, they had the imported ketchup that didn't run. The insignificant things we normally take for granted had now noticeably become small luxuries.

After we were safe inside, I called Ben from the embassy's pay phone and gave him the horrible news about Freda and the attack on our office building. He expressed his shock and anger and said that he would try to notify Freda's family and the rest of the employees.

Ben also mentioned that he would inform all the employees to meet at our office building in the morning if possible. This depended entirely on things quieting down and on our building still standing.

It was now just getting dark, and downtown had become eerily quiet. There was even a lull with the traffic on the streets. It was It was if all the hooligans, arsonists, and revolutionists had all gotten tired and gone home to rest up from their busy day. Bill and I saw this pause as a good opportunity to leave the embassy, and we both scurried to the safety of our homes.

The next morning, I cautiously walked to work as the lingering smoke from the still-smoldering buildings assaulted my senses. It was peaceful enough, as if an uneasy calm had descended on the downtown streets. I observed small groups of people wandering around in a hushed silence as they pointed out the destruction to each other.

When I reached our office building, I was relieved to see that it had not gone up in flames as many of the others had. The civilian employees of the Iranian air force were already busy sweeping up the broken glass and cleaning up the ashes and rubble in the lobby.

I could just see a charred corner of the Shah's gilded picture frame glinting in the debris. The revolutionaries had piled the wooden lobby furniture near the stairwell as planned and then doused it with naft before lighting it. The resulting heat had caused the marble tiles to buckle and the cement floor to swell slightly.

I ran up to the third floor without stopping, as I had to satisfy my curiosity concerning what was burned on that floor. The cafeteria appeared intact, but upon further investigation, I could see that the Iranian air force executive dining room had been their target. This richly olivewood-paneled room with its heavily carved wooden rococo furnishings now lay in ruin. The executive dining room had been an obvious target as the Farsi sign on the door identified the room as the *Otageh Shah* (King's Room). As I had satisfied my curiosity, I returned back to our offices on the second floor.

Our office building escaped burning because it was constructed primarily of steel and masonry with little in the building that was flammable. There were no carpets or suspended ceilings, and our office furniture was the wood-grained metal kind that was readily available on the Iranian market. Even the miniblinds covering our windows were made of metal. In addition, in their haste, the revolutionists had failed to break any upstairs windows, which would have created an upward draft for the flames to travel up the stairwell. Other than the fire damage sustained in the lobby and the executive dining room, the only other damage inflicted was from the thick, black smoke.

By this time, all of the other employees had arrived and gathered in the area outside Ben's office. He had notified everyone by telephone about Freda's passing, but he had been unable to reach her family. He announced that we would have a service for her at ten o'clock in the conference room next to his office.

Everyone was in shock about Freda's death and naturally wanted to know the details of what had happened after they had left our offices yesterday. Bill and I repeatedly told our stories and answered their questions. We then busied ourselves by cleaning up the black soot that had settled over everything. If you brushed up against anything, you would have to pay with a black smudge left behind on your clothing.

I had just put down my blackened dust cloth when I felt a sudden compulsion to go to the photocopy room. I thought this was strange, as I had earlier vowed never to enter that room again. However, I soon found myself on the way there as though I had been summoned. I entered the room and relived the tragic events of yesterday as I stared out the window at the villa's grounds below.

Just as I was ready to leave, I felt a bizarre sensation, as if someone was lightly breathing on the back of my neck. I quickly turned around and saw the transparent ghostly apparition of Freda wearing her black chador. We made eye contact, and I looked into her radiant smiling face as she quickly faded away. She didn't speak a single word, but I knew she had told me not to worry because she was in good hands. As she disappeared, I realized it was almost time for the service to begin.

I was the last to enter the conference room where all the other employees were already seated around the rectangular wooden table. Mary had just placed a perfect white rose in a clear bud vase on the table in front of Freda's conspicuously vacant chair just to the right of Ben. Mary and Freda were clearly Ben's favorites, as he always presided at the head of the conference table during staff meetings with Freda on his right and Mary on his left.

Mary had obviously purloined the rose from one of the many beautiful flower gardens scattered throughout the city. The Persians loved their flowers, and because of the high, dry climate, most did quite well in Tehran. They even named their oldest historic monument, the Golestan Palace, in honor of a flower garden. In Farsi, *gol* means flower and *estan* means place of, which translates in English as place of the flowers or flower garden.

Most colonels were good at public speaking from their years of military experience, and Ben was no exception. He had come prepared with a poignant prayer for Freda followed by his presentation of a touching eulogy. Then, one by one, each employee in turn, stood up and personally eulogized Freda.

When it came my turn, I wanted to share my ghost story with everyone at the service. But I knew if I did this, some of the employees, including Ben, would probably think the stress was getting to me. However, I simply didn't care what they thought. I had to tell them anyway.

I stood up and began to speak. "I know some of you are not going to believe this, but I was just summoned to the photocopy room by the ghost of Freda. She wants you all to know she is safe and in good hands."

Everyone started asking their questions all at once, wanting to know in detail exactly what had happened during my spiritual encounter. I started answering their questions and then glanced down at Ben. He was clearly giving me the eye and looked a little irritated that I had interrupted the decorum of Freda's service. I then knew it was time to move on and doubted that Ben believed in ghosts anyway. I continued with my eulogy concerning the time Freda represented me in court after a traffic accident.

It happened early one Saturday morning not long after I had first arrived in Tehran. I was driving my jeep westward on Elizabeth Boulevard, a four-lane street separated by a wide landscaped median that was named in honor of Queen Elizabeth I.

I was on my way to the part of town where all the vehicle repair shops were clustered and had left early to avoid the traffic. My jeep had an oil filter gasket that was leaking. I either wanted to buy a replacement or find a sheet of cork gasket material and make it myself.

I took a left off Elizabeth through the median to head south on the cross street that led to the repair shops. As I passed through the median, I looked to the right for approaching traffic in the opposing two lanes. I could just see a vehicle coming over the crest of the small hill. There seemed to be plenty of time for me to cross, but I had mistakenly misjudged the excessive speed of the approaching car.

The speeding vehicle, a 1965 Volvo sedan, clipped the right-rear side of my jeep, which resulted in it being spun around in a clockwise direction. The violent collision caused me to be ejected out of the canvas door onto the pavement of the busy street. I landed on my backside and then rolled onto my left wrist. The jeep continued over the curb and onto the sidewalk where it came to a stop.

I was in shock but still had enough sense to get out of the street and sit down on the grassy median. A curious crowd quickly gathered, and some expressed their sympathy for my swollen wrist. Luckily, none of the six people riding in the Volvo were injured.

A uniformed policeman appeared shortly after the accident, and I gave him my driver's license. He spoke with the other driver and then wrote me a ticket. I stood there feeling helpless, as I did not understand their conversation and couldn't say anything in my own defense. I could not even read the ticket that he handed to me.

Fortunately, the damage to my sturdy jeep was minimal, but the right-front fender of the Volvo was totally smashed. The policeman allowed me to leave, and I carefully drove home.

The next day I was sore with my bruises and contusions, but I went to work. There was nothing broken, and I saw no need to stay home. When I arrived at the office, I told Ben what had happened and showed him the ticket I had received. He then summoned Freda over the intercom to come to his office and translate my ticket.

Freda read the ticket and said I had been summoned to be in court by ten o'clock that morning. She also said I would need to take cash with me to pay any fines or damages levied against me. Fortunately, I had recently replenished the petty cash fund to its maximum authorized value of ten thousand riyals. With Ben's permission, I raided my safe of all the cash. Freda and I then grabbed Albert and rushed off to court.

We arrived at the traffic court building shortly before ten o'clock. It was a two-story stucco building fronted with a pair of glass double doors opening directly into the small courtroom from the street. We entered the building and could see a presiding judge holding court at the opposite end of the room. There seemed to be little order, as there was a crowd of people milling around the judge's elevated bench waiting for their cases to be heard. We signed in at a desk just to the right of the front doors and joined the crowd.

When it came my turn, Freda turned on her charm and did her best to argue on my behalf. The entire proceeding was in Farsi, and I could only understand a few words.

As the judge spoke with the plaintiff, I whispered to Freda, "Freda, what's happening?"

She replied to me quietly with her hand cupped over her mouth. "Well, John-Boy, it doesn't look good. I argued that the plaintiff's oncoming vehicle was responsible for the accident, as it was traveling at an excessive rate of speed. But there is no proof of his undue speed, and he has denied speeding at all. The judge is going to issue his ruling now."

The judge then laughed and appeared to joke with Freda as he issued his decision.

Freda then turned to me and said, "The judge has ruled against you, stating you caused the accident by turning left in front of the plaintiff's vehicle. You must pay for the damages."

"How much are the damages?" I quickly asked.

"They are discussing it now," she answered. "The plaintiff wants eight thousand riyals, and the judge has just agreed with him. Give me eight thousand riyals."

I then counted out the cash and handed it to Freda. She, in turn, passed it to the judge, and he gave it to the plaintiff. The judge chose not to levy a fine against me, and there were no court costs involved. The matter had been adjudicated, and I was free to go.

On our way back to the office, I could not help but feel a little down about the whole thing. But I felt better about it as Freda laughed and joked, calling the judge improper. I didn't ask what she meant, because I knew better than to ask a question if I couldn't stand the answer. But my spirits were lifted anyway until we arrived back at the office. I then had to write a personal check for eight thousand riyals to reimburse the company's petty cash fund.

After the service, Ben announced his news that he had earlier confided to me. He now explained to all of us that he had been in contact with the air force attaché who was assigned to the embassy. The attaché informed Ben that the US Air Force would have a daily C-130 flight round-trip between the air base just outside Athens and Tehran. This flight would continue for as long as possible, and there was space available for all of us. We only had to sign up on the log sheet, and Mary would then make the reservations through the embassy.

Ben also announced that our contractor in Isfahan had been issued a suspension of work, stop-work order by our management in Fort Worth, ceasing all work on our helicopter-manufacturing facility. The contractor had requested permission to continue pouring a section of the foundation which was currently work in progress. Permission was denied, and the contractor was instructed not to incur any additional construction costs.

I knew I should leave Tehran as soon as possible, so I signed up for the flight leaving the very next day. Mary and I were the only employees who wanted to leave that soon. Everyone else had personal matters to tie up before departing. Ben said we should arrive at the motor-pool entrance of the embassy by eight o'clock in the morning, and they would provide secured transportation to the airport for all departing expatriates.

After the meeting, Ben pulled me aside and confided in me. "I'll be leaving Shell soon after things are wrapped up here. I've landed a manager-level job in administration at the US embassy here in Tehran."

It was common knowledge that our embassy was heavily staffed with retired military, as they were given preference because of their experience and training. Due to the revolution, there was a high turnover of personnel at the embassy. I was sure some of Ben's retired military acquaintances working at the embassy had given him some assistance in the matter.

I then replied with a little envy. "That's great news, Ben. Good for you. Just thinking I'll be looking for employment soon myself, and I wouldn't mind working at the embassy. Let me know if a good job opens up in your area. You have my stateside information."

"I'll certainly do that," Ben said and then added, "Before I forget about it, I just wanted to tell you not to worry about the money we're leaving behind at the Bank of Rotterdam."

I suddenly felt a twinge of guilt, as I had never informed Ben that I had managed to withdraw the money and close out the company's account.

I then asked, "Really? Why is that?"

Ben then explained. "Shell is better off abandoning the money in the bank account, as it can be claimed against the contract-termination provision that was funded in advance. The company could then add its labor burdens and profit margin onto the $253,000 and actually make a tidy sum."

I now realized why my management in Fort Worth didn't seem too concerned about leaving the money behind.

Ben then further confided. "In my opinion, the company should have terminated our contract for cause and safely pulled its people out months ago. However, our contract is a cost-plus type that reimbursed the company for its incurred cost and then allowed it to apply its burdens and margin on top of it. The longer the company kept its people in Iran, the more cost would be incurred, and the more money the company would make."

I replied in a joking manner, "Well, those sorry rascals!"

The wheels of temptation were now in motion as I thought to myself, *Well, if that's the case, the $253,000 is now mine, and it will be the perfect crime. No one knows about the money, and the company doesn't even want it back. The Bank of Rotterdam has closed its doors, and its records of the transaction are soon to be blown away by the winds of the revolution. More importantly, I now have a way out of the country.*

I knew, though, I would have to run with the money with my head held like a common thief in the night. There would be no escape from the shame and guilt that I would feel deep inside from the crime I was about to commit. Without a doubt, I would have to bear this heavy yoke for the rest of my life. I had now surrendered to the will of darkness without even so much as a struggle, and I couldn't care less.

The next morning I woke up early and prepared to leave. I knew it was best if I traveled as light as possible, so I planned to take only my suitcase and a small backpack. My backpack contained only a few toiletries, my rabbit's foot keychain, my camera, and a change of clothing. I hoped to get some good pictures of the C-130 evacuation flight.

But like the Shah with his container of soil, I too had to take a small part of Iran with me, and what better souvenir than my ninth-century Persian oil lamp? I had a small cardboard box that would snuggly hold the little lamp, and I used crumpled tissue as packing material to protect it from harm's way. There was even enough room for it in my backpack.

I then gave my apartment a final walk-through, and everything seemed to be in order. I didn't tell my landlord I was leaving. I wasn't too concerned about this, as I had initially put up a one-month rent deposit, which I would now be forfeiting. Also, I would be leaving behind all of my furniture, appliances, personal possessions, carpets, and even my handcrafted Afghan teapot. Earlier I had considered selling my furnishings and appliances but decided against it. I just didn't feel comfortable with unknown strangers coming inside my home to look at the items I had for sale.

As I left my apartment to walk down to the embassy, it was just getting light. I could now hear the loudspeakers in the downtown mosques calling the faithful to prayer. I then passed a beet vendor on the corner just setting up his charcoal-heated, black metal cart to sell his steaming hot beet slices. You always knew autumn had arrived in Tehran when the beet vendors showed up on the streets of downtown. They typically stayed throughout the winter and seemed to disappear at the first signs of spring.

Upon arriving at the embassy's rear motor-pool gate, I could see a small convoy parked on the street. The convoy consisted of two powder-blue Mercedes minibuses being escorted by an Iranian armored army jeep in the front and one in the rear. The front jeep was manned by a driver, a gunner, and a lieutenant who was in charge of the operation. The rear jeep had only a driver and a gunner. Both had a .30-caliber Browning machine gun mounted in the rear of each vehicle.

I had just signed in on the passenger manifest when I saw Shapour arriving for work. He was an Iranian waiter who had worked for the American embassy's dining facility for many years. When we ate at the embassy, we would normally sit at a booth along the front windows. Shapour usually waited on this area and always greeted us with a friendly smile. He usually spoke to us in Farsi, and I always enjoyed the good-natured practice. It was a nice surprise to see Shapour before departing.

When Shapour saw me, he smiled and waved. "*Ahgahyeh Saybill, halle tu coubeh?*" (Mister Moustache, how is your health?)

I laughed as I replied, "Hi, *Bow-Bow! Coubam merci, hamishay coubam! Shomah coubeed?*" (Hi, Grandpa! I am good thanks, always good! Are you well?)

Shapour then replied in a more subdued tone. "*Coubam merci, alon yek kami metarzam, Ayatollah meyahd.*" (I am good thanks, but now I am a little worried—the Ayatollah comes.)

Shapour had a good reason to be concerned, because he had served the US government faithfully for many years in, of all places, its embassy. Once the conservative right had their way and the cleansing process began, I wondered if the intensity of their retribution would reach down to his level.

I really could find no words of encouragement for him. There I was, an American who was lucky enough to be leaving. Then there was Shapour who, like millions of others, had to stay behind and face an uncertain future at the hands of the revolutionaries. I shook his hand, said good-bye, and wished him good luck before boarding the bus.

Mary arrived shortly afterward and took the next vacant seat toward the rear of the bus. Both busses were soon filled to capacity, and our little armored convoy left the American embassy promptly at eight o'clock for the Mehrabad International Airport. It was about a forty-five-minute drive to the west.

I soon settled into my seat and fell into my usual habit of practicing my Farsi by translating the commercial signs along the street. This wasn't difficult, as most commercial signs were written first in Farsi and then followed with the English translation below.

There are few places in the world outside Iran and Afghanistan where this language is spoken. I couldn't help but feel a little amused, as I was practicing it on the way to the airport for a one-way exit out of the country.

The main gate at Mehrabad International Airport appeared on the left side of the minibus. We slowed down with the traffic at the gate but strangely enough continued straight ahead instead of turning into the left-turn lane to enter the airport. As we passed by the entrance gate, everyone in the bus turned their heads in unison and watched uneasily as the gate got smaller in the distance.

I could now see the angst written on my fellow passengers' faces as they glanced around the bus at each other and expressed their concern in whispers. The man sitting in the seat next to me had spoken when he first sat down but had since remained silent.

With a concerned look on his face, he now asked, "Did you tune into the BBC this morning?"

I inquisitively answered, "No, I didn't. Why, what happened?"

I had been concerned with departing, so I hadn't taken the time to listen to the news. I now regretted having left my portable shortwave Sony radio behind.

"The BBC had an unconfirmed report that an entire garrison of the Iranian army had mutinied in Tehran," he explained. "These troops are now loyal to the opposition."

I now understood the worried look on his face. This sort of news always traveled quickly among the expatriates. I was sure by now that almost everyone onboard was aware of this development and had at least silently questioned the loyalty of our army escorts.

We then continued straight ahead for more than a mile and turned left toward a large, undeveloped area just south of the airport. I was familiar with this locale, as I had taken my jeep four-wheeling over the windswept rough terrain on more than one occasion.

Usually you could see several groups of rural herders camped out in their low-slung tents with their flocks of sheep on their way to the market. But because of the revolution, the livestock market had closed, and the area now remained completely vacant.

I couldn't help but continue to be concerned as to why we didn't enter Mehrabad's main gate. Now, for some unknown reason, we were headed toward the desolate area behind the airport.

I tried to rationally dismiss these thoughts as being nothing more than an overreaction to a fear of the unknown, but they still remained with me. We then abruptly came to a stop at a T intersection opposite the vacant expanse and waited for the oncoming traffic to pass.

Instead of turning left toward the rear of the airport or right to the west, our little caravan proceeded straight ahead through the intersection and left the pavement onto the hard, sandy soil. We continued on a straight course for a short distance until we came to a large sandstone bluff where we turned left toward the east. Our caravan then came to a sudden halt. All four vehicles were now parked in a single row parallel to both the distant road on the left and the imposing nearby rocky bluff on our right.

I now turned around in my seat and saw the concerned faces of Mary and my other fellow passengers as the first lieutenant quickly boarded the bus. He promptly raised his hand and smiled as if to reassure and calm the passengers before speaking. I then saw his nice, wide smile and realized it seemed hauntingly familiar. As a matter of fact, it looked just like the smile I had seen on the lieutenant's masked face in my nightmare as he examined the bundle of riyals.

He then began to speak in flawless English, and I was astounded that not only did he have the same smile, but he also had the same voice as my assailant. I then noticed the heat he was packing, a .38-caliber, stainless-steel revolver. Just a coincidence, or was my dream now becoming reality? I wasn't so sure any more.

Everyone was totally silent and listened carefully. "My apologies to everyone, as there will be a slight delay of not more than a half hour," the lieutenant announced. "Because of security concerns, the air force has forbidden our minibuses to enter the airport."

Mehrabad International Airport was a civilian airport that was shared with the Iranian air force, and its security was always of utmost concern.

He continued. "The Iranian air force is now sending a secured military bus large enough to hold all of you. We need your help to unload the luggage, and then you must form a line parallel to both our caravan and the adjacent bluff. An orderly line will facilitate the timely loading of the incoming bus."

The officer then left our vehicle, and I could hear him making the same announcement on the second bus.

We lined up like mindless sheep with our luggage by our sides. We thought nothing about it, because as Americans, lining up was a cultural thing that had to do with efficiency and fairness that we had all learned at an early age. We even have rules for the line that are expected to be observed. The Iranians, however, rarely lined up for anything, usually preferring just to crowd around and jostle with each other for a better position toward the front.

Because I helped unload the luggage, I was the last one in the line from our bus. The passengers from the second bus then entered the line behind me and I now found myself exactly in the middle.

I was just chatting with the older man to my left when I heard a woman behind him gasp and excitably exclaim, "*Look! Look at that! Oh my God!*"

I glanced up and could see that the lieutenant and his men were now all wearing the same black ski masks of the executioners in my dream. I also noticed that the muzzles of the .30-caliber machine guns mounted on the backs of the jeeps had been lowered and were now aimed at the opposite ends of the line.

The lieutenant was holding his pistol in his right hand pointed upward. He then fired it into the air as if to get our undivided attention, and in English quickly issued his command. "Ready, aim, *fire!*" The carnage began at both ends of the line as the machine guns began firing and in seemingly slow motion swept toward me in the middle. I could no longer hear their cries as I silently wondered what it would be like to die. It must be a spiritual experience, but would I see the same bright white light associated with near-death experiences? Maybe I would see the loving faces of my deceased relatives, or perhaps the power would simply be switched off and I would see nothing at all.

I didn't know the answer to this, but I did know my time was growing near, and I did not want to die alone. So I closed my eyes and held a deep breath as I summoned all of my loved ones, all of my friends and family, to be with me by my side during my time of need.

They all came as I requested, and I bravely accepted my fate. I now had nothing to fear, as I knew I was going home. When the line of machine gun fire reached the two people on either side of me, I suddenly blinked my eyes several times as the minibus hit a pothole and quickly snapped out of my daydream!

My familiar companion, my adventurous imaginary alter ego, was now safely tucked away until the next time. I was relieved to see the gated rear entrance of the airport coming up on the left side of the bus.

The Iranian air force guards at the airport's rear gate were obviously expecting us as they quickly opened the gate and waved us through. Our caravan proceeded to the first of two east-west runways and came to a sudden halt before crossing it. We waited for what seem like forever before a fully armed Iranian air force F4 Phantom fighter jet touched down with a loud roar just in front of us.

The F4s had been circling the downtown area in an obvious show of force for the past several days. We were all relieved the air force had continued to remain loyal to the government. Our caravan then proceeded across the second runway without incident. We could now see the distant US Air Force C-130 parked alone on the tarmac at the isolated northwest corner of the airport.

As we slowly proceeded toward the C-130, I couldn't help but feel a bit humbled as I proudly saw the American flag displayed on the aircraft's vertical stabilizer. Our caravan then pulled up and stopped adjacent to the aircraft.

The young but capable loadmaster from the C-130 boarded our bus and took a head count. He instructed us to unload our luggage and wait outside the aircraft until given permission to board through the open rear door. We all complied with his instructions and were met by a waiting representative from the American embassy. He then proceeded to take down each passenger's name, passport number, Social Security number, stateside address, and next of kin. He advised that we would not be charged by the US government for our priceless journey.

Shortly afterward, at exactly 9:30, we were curious to see an Air France 747 touch down on the runway just in front of us and taxi to the main terminal. We thought all commercial aircraft were now forbidden to fly in Iranian airspace to prevent the Ayatollah from returning from France. But if that were true, then how could this be happening? We could only imagine the moment in history we had just witnessed.

We then expected to board the aircraft shortly and be on our way to peace and tranquility in Athens. But we waited and waited in the glaring sun without any explanation until early morning slowly became early afternoon. We finally realized that this aircraft had another mission other than just our evacuation.

Americans waiting to board a US Air Force C-130 evacuation flight at Mehrabad International Airport

As we all chatted about the reason for the delay, a flatbed truck pulled up with two large plywood crates on its bed. We didn't have a clue about what was in the crates, but our speculations ranged from sensitive military equipment to the ambassador's household furnishings.

We then watched as the mystery crates were offloaded with a large forklift. The forklift gently deposited the crates on the reclining rear door of the C-130. They were slowly winched up the ball-bearing surface of the open rear door one by one into the aircraft's fuselage toward the front. When both crates were finally loaded and secured, the loadmaster signaled that all was clear. We were then instructed to board the airplane up the steps on the right side of the same rear doorway with our luggage in hand.

As we boarded the aircraft, there was just enough room to squeeze between the two large wooden crates in the middle and the orange nylon sling seats attached to the sides of the aircraft. As I was one of the first to board, I selected a good seat on the left side near the front where I could turn my head to the left and see directly up the steps into the open cockpit.

Other passengers weren't as lucky, as they would have to be seated facing the wooden crates for the entire flight. The only space we had for our luggage was under the orange nylon straps of our seats or in the middle of the fuselage not occupied by the wooden crates. I couldn't help but feel a little uneasy as there were no seat belts. But we were getting out, and that was all that really mattered.

Mary and an air force C-130 crewmember

We then taxied to the adjacent runway and quickly became airborne to the east over downtown. As we lifted off, there was a jubilant round of applause and cheering. This elation soon turned to a moment of sobering silence as we now observed the downtown area continuing to burn below.

The aircraft circled around through a pall of black smoke to a westward heading toward Athens for the three-hour flight. Our destination was the US Air Force Hellenikon Air Base at the Athinai Airport just outside of Athens.

CHAPTER V

I now relaxed and smiled to myself as I remembered that it was February 1. The prophecies of the notes left on my jeep's windshield and the threatening graffiti written on the wall had indeed both come true.

The overhead lights were turned off shortly after takeoff, and the interior night lighting was turned on as darkness descended on our flight. The luminosity of the cockpit combined with the dim night lighting cast an almost surreal glow on the interior of the aircraft with its two large wooden crates surrounded by grateful Americans and their luggage.

Americans onboard a C-130 evacuation flight from Tehran to Athens

I couldn't help but think to myself that there was more than just the lighting that seemed unreal. Here I was being evacuated from the Iranian Revolution on a US Air Force C-130 with my nylon sling seat being cushioned by a cool quarter million in cash. I knew things couldn't get much better.

The crew onboard the flight had no food to share but was able to offer us water. We were all grateful for that, as we had spent most of the day waiting in the hot sun. In the dim light, I could see the shadowy figures of the other passengers as some nodded off to sleep. However, most were still awake like me. I thought of the entire flight as a once-in-a-lifetime adventure that was just too exciting to miss by sleeping through it. From my seat, I stayed awake and watched all the activity through the open cockpit door as the crew went through their paces flying us to Athens.

The C-130 landed at the air base shortly after seven and was promptly met by a waiting military bus. We were transported directly to the nearby Apollo Palace Hotel where the air force had reserved a block of rooms for us.

The Apollo Palace is a 290-room, eight-story seaside resort hotel along the scenic Saronic Gulf near Athens. As we arrived at the hotel, I was relieved that we never had to process through Greek customs. Once we landed, we were never subjected to any scrutiny by either the Greek authorities or the American military.

I walked into the hotel lobby and noticed an open travel agency office across the lobby. As tempted as I was to spend a few days relaxing in this beautiful hotel, I knew I should leave Athens as soon as possible. It was just too risky for me to leave my bag of money sitting alone in a hotel room for any length of time.

I inquired at the travel agency about flights leaving the next day for the United States. All of the westbound flights were already booked, but the travel agent was able to find space available on an eastbound Pan Pacific Airlines flight. This flight was scheduled to leave Athens International Airport at 10:10 the next morning. It would then fly to Istanbul before refueling in Osaka. The flight would finally terminate in Honolulu. The travel agent offered me a 5 percent discount for the coach fare. Without hesitation, I bought the ticket and then checked in at the front desk.

I was pleasantly surprised as I checked out my beautiful room on the eighth floor with a balcony overlooking the blue waters of the gulf. However, I had not eaten for the entire day and could now feel the emptiness in my stomach. I concealed my suitcase as usual under the bed before taking the elevator downstairs to try out some authentic Greek food.

I always enjoyed eating the local cuisine from the street vendors, and that day was no exception. I only had a short walk from the hotel before I came across Zorba's Grill, a small restaurant with an open counter on the street selling its authentic Greek food to go. I placed an order for chicken *souvlas* with *dolmades* and *patates tiganites*. This translated as chicken kebab with stuffed grape leaves and fried potatoes.

The proprietor handed me the food and a bottle of pomegranate juice. I was then attracted by a brightly lit building down the street. As I ate with my hands full, I walked toward the light and could soon see that it was actually the neon marquee of a movie theater. When I got close enough, I could see that the name of the movie on the marquee was *Grease*.

Imagine that, here I was in Greece, and there was an American movie playing with the curious name of *Grease*. As I read the movie poster inside the glass front case, I wondered about the acting and musical ability of the unknown headliner John Travolta. I was also concerned whether the movie was subtitled or dubbed in Greek.

I quickly realized that the dialogue of a musical would probably not be dubbed in Greek and would most likely have subtitles instead. I finished up with the last of my souvlas and bought my ticket for the final ten o'clock showing. Just to be on the safe side, I confirmed at that time that the movie was actually in English.

I entered the almost-empty theater, selected a good seat in the middle, and for almost two hours I was taken back to America. For this short period of time, I was totally absorbed in this movie and was no longer concerned about the revolution or the bag of money sitting alone in my hotel room. I left the movie that night in good spirits and hummed the sounds of the title track all the way back to my hotel.

It seemed that I had hardly fallen asleep when I heard a ringing off in the distance that continued to get louder and louder. I opened my eyes and realized that it was the wake-up call I had requested upon returning from the movie. I answered the call and then quickly jumped up and showered, knowing that I could not be late for my flight. I was appreciative for the one change of clothing I had brought along.

I glanced around the room, making sure that I had not forgotten anything before taking the elevator downstairs and checking out at the front desk. I then took one of the Mercedes taxis waiting in line just outside the lobby to the Pan Pacific Airlines counter at the Athens International Airport.

After standing in line for about a half hour at the Pan Pacific Airlines counter, I finally reached the ticket agent where I presented my ticket and passport for a boarding pass. I then explained to the agent I didn't want to check my suitcase but wanted to carry it on instead. I felt it would be best if I could stow it where I could at least keep my eye on it.

She replied I would be flying on a Boeing 707 and that my suitcase was too large to fit in the open overheads. There were no closeable storage bins above the seating on the aircraft. I reluctantly agreed and said good-bye to my little suitcase of money as I watched it disappear down the conveyer belt, knowing I wouldn't see it again until we reached Honolulu. I then proceeded to passport control, relieved my suitcase had not been searched.

I boarded the 707 and slowly made my way past the other boarding passengers to my window seat at the left rear of the aircraft. On my way to the back, I couldn't help but think that this aircraft must be one of the older ones left in service as I noticed the obvious signs of wear to the interior. When I arrived at my seat, I saw that the frayed upholstery on my worn armrest had been repaired by wrapping duct tape around it. Looking at this repair job, I couldn't help but worry about the mechanical condition of the aircraft. I crossed my fingers and hoped for the best.

We took off as scheduled, and after about forty-five minutes of flight time, the aging 707 shuddered as the flaps were extended and the landing gears lowered. We then began our final approach to the Istanbul Ataturk Airport. I looked out the window and observed a sea of red tile roofs surrounding the airport with the narrow Bosporus Straits in the distance. The landing was uneventful, and we quickly taxied to our gate.

For a number of passengers, Istanbul was their final destination, and they deplaned quickly. An equal number of new passengers then boarded, filling the aircraft back to its capacity. We would shortly be bound for Honolulu via a brief refueling stop in Osaka.

As the new passengers boarded, I noticed among them an Iranian man dressed in an expensive brown woolen suit. It was a suit tailored with flared legs that I recognized as being fashionable in Tehran. His aisle seat was in the row in front of me and just to the right. After he got settled in his seat, he began reading the Farsi edition of the *Daily Kayhan*, whose headlines had obvious news of the revolution.

At that time I didn't know what had happened in Iran since leaving Tehran the day before. My curiosity was getting the best of me. I had just gotten out of my seat to ask him if the Ayatollah Khomeini had made his return when I saw a female passenger carrying an *International Herald Tribune* newspaper onboard.

The *International Herald Tribune* is the global voice of the *New York Times*. It is a trusted source of English-language news and is widely read and respected by American expatriates working overseas.

She had obviously already read it inside the terminal and had now brought it onboard to share with the other passengers. As she put the folded newspaper in the magazine rack at the front of the cabin, I raced up there to grab it before anyone else did. I then returned to my seat and put the newspaper away in my seat pocket, determined not to read it until after the meal was served and the overhead lights had dimmed.

All of the new passengers had completed their boarding, and I thought we would soon taxi to the runway when I noticed something unusual. I looked out my window and saw that our luggage was now being offloaded from the airplane and lined up on the tarmac.

The captain then made an announcement in French, which I couldn't understand, followed with an English version. I had to listen carefully as he stated that each passenger would have to exit the aircraft using the rear exit and identify their luggage before boarding again up the stairway in the front of the aircraft.

This was the first time I had ever experienced something like this. I could not understand why they were unloading our luggage until it occurred to me it must have something to do with my suitcase full of money. But how could the Turks know what was in my suitcase? After all, we had just landed in Turkey. Maybe a dog had sniffed it out, or perhaps they randomly searched it for some reason. I just didn't know.

In growing apprehension, I stared out the window with wide eyes, my attention riveted on my green vinyl suitcase. It was now lined up on the tarmac with the rest of the passengers' luggage.

The passengers began to line up at the rear exit, and I watched through the window as they each descended the stairway and identified their baggage. The luggage handlers then put each bag on the cart to be reloaded on the aircraft. As instructed, the passengers reentered the aircraft up the stairway, through the front entrance, and back to their seats.

I had just gotten up from my seat to join the diminishing line when I felt the sudden urge to visit the restroom. I quickly ducked into the vacant toilet just to the rear of my seat and took a nervous pee. I then flushed and pondered my fate at the hands of the Turks as I watched the blue sanitizing liquid swirl down the toilet.

I knew the Turks were not to be taken lightly. For some reason, I instinctively knew to be wary of them. It was nothing I could put my finger on, but while in Tehran, I had seen the recently released movie *Midnight Express*, which graphically detailed the cruelty of the Turkish prison system. Perhaps it was this movie that sowed the seeds of my newly acquired fear of the Turks.

I quickly washed my hands and splashed some water on my face as if the act of doing so would somehow relieve my pain. As my pulse began to quicken, I gathered all my courage, opened the door, and stepped into the cabin.

As I entered the cabin, I noticed that the line of passengers had disappeared down the stairway, and I would be the last one to join them. I then conspicuously entered the end of the line and watched as the remaining passengers in front of me identified their luggage and proceeded to the front of the aircraft to board again.

When it came my turn to identify my bag, there were only two left—my green one and a black canvas bag to its right. It occurred to me that I could identify the black bag as being my own, and I would then that have nothing to worry about. But if I did that, I would definitely have to say good-bye to my $253,000. No thanks. I'd just have to take my chances. After all, none of the other passengers had had any problems, and the entire procedure had gone smoothly.

As I stepped forward to identify my bag, I couldn't help but feel the aura of an unknown menacing presence behind me. When I identified my bag by touching it, two mustachioed men dressed in dark blue police uniforms stepped up from the rear and firmly grabbed my upper arms on both sides.

I quickly glanced at both of them and could see that they were wearing the uniform insignia of the airport police. I was astounded as the sergeant on my right handcuffed me and said in perfect English with a thick Turkish accent, "You are under arrest! Surrender your passport and come with us!"

In total disbelief and shock over what was happening, I handed over my passport while protesting. "I'm under arrest? For what? Why are you arresting me? Where are you taking me? You can't do this!"

The two officers paid no attention to my protests and didn't bother to answer as they accompanied me, along with my backpack and suitcase, inside the terminal building to the nearby airport police station. We then proceeded to a small, brightly lit room constructed of unpainted cinder blocks and furnished only with a metal card table and two folding chairs. I knew this room was used for interrogations, as it had a two-way mirror built into the wall just opposite my chair.

The officers left me alone and locked me inside the interrogation room for the next hour to raise the level of my anxiety and soften me up for the impending interview. During this time, I remained cuffed and sat uncomfortably, facing my reflection in the two-way mirror.

My imaginary second self had just picked a fight with the tattooed bully inside the unforgiving walls of the mean Turkish prison when the sergeant suddenly unlocked the door and entered the room with my suitcase. He then opened it on the table in front of me and released me from the handcuffs.

The officer introduced himself only by his first name, Mustafa, and sat down in the opposite chair. He then produced my passport, which he had confiscated after my arrest, and proceeded to carefully examine all the information, paying particular attention to the custom stamps on the visa pages.

He then initiated the interrogation by asking, "Mr. Tipton, where did you get this money?"

I looked him straight in the eye and with an air of self-confidence answered, "This is my company's money, and I'm returning it to the Shell Helicopter Company in Fort Worth, Texas. Because of the Iranian Revolution, I had to close out our account in Tehran, and the bank paid me in riyals."

I then showed him my company identification and the copy of the Bank of Rotterdam's check along with my signature on the account closure documents.

"When did you leave Tehran?" he asked.

"I departed Tehran on the first of February," I replied

Mustafa rubbed his forehead and said, "Mr. Tipton, I am unable to find an Iranian exit stamp on the visa pages of your passport indicating your departure on the first. Where did you really get this money?"

I suddenly felt uncomfortable and squirmed in my seat as I replied, "I was evacuated from Tehran on a US Air Force C-130 flight to Athens because the commercial air traffic in Iran had been grounded. I don't have an exit stamp because I didn't process through Iranian customs."

He then said in a sarcastic tone, "Really? Do you understand you've been charged with smuggling?"

It immediately flashed through my mind that smuggling was the exact same charge filed by the Turkish authorities in *Midnight Express*. I answered in stunned disbelief. "I've been charged with smuggling? That's impossible, because I'm a passenger in transit. I never processed through Turkish customs and entered your country. If I never entered Turkey, how could I possibly be charged with smuggling?"

"Mr. Tipton," he said, "you entered this country when you stepped off that airplane onto Turkish soil. You have been charged with smuggling because you violated Turkish currency laws when you took possession of your bag of money without declaring its content."

As the interview proceeded, it was evident that this cop was tainted and had only one thing in mind—how to separate me from my money. I couldn't believe I was being railroaded like this without even the benefit of an attorney to defend me. They didn't even bother to read me my rights. *How ironic,* I thought. *It's now the thief stealing from the thief.*

Mustafa continued. "I'm prepared to offer you a deal. If you agree to plead guilty to the smuggling charge, you will only have to forfeit your contraband. There will then be a small fine, and you will be allowed to proceed on your way. But if you choose to plead not guilty, then you will have to stand trial and run the risk of not only losing your money but also your freedom."

I couldn't think of a good response to such a raw deal while suddenly having to worry about my freedom, which had just been threatened. I instinctively circled the wagons and replied defensively by saying only, "You're nuts, Mustafa!"

But it was getting late, and it was now time for the sergeant to end his shift. I had not given up my position and could tell that Mustafa was growing impatient with me. He said I should sleep on it, and we would continue the interview in the morning.

I was then escorted down the hallway to a nearby holding cell. As I heard the steel door slam shut behind me, I was suddenly jolted back to reality. I now watched as the last of the blue sanitizing liquid flushed down the aircraft's toilet. I could not help but feel that my imaginary alter ego had somehow momentarily slipped into a fleeting imaginary time lapse.

While attempting to better understand my baffling enigma, I quickly left the restroom, not bothering to wash my hands, and joined the end of the line down the stairway. When it came time for me to identify my bag, there were only two left. Oddly enough, there was my green valise with the black canvas bag to the right of it—just as I had imagined.

I knew, regardless of the consequences, I had to bravely select my little suitcase.

I identified it as mine, and it was immediately loaded onboard the cart by the luggage handlers to be reloaded on the aircraft. The black bag was whisked off in the opposite direction toward the terminal. I then quickly proceeded to the front of the aircraft and boarded up the stairway.

I had just returned to my seat when the captain made another announcement as before, first in French and followed by English. He apologized for the delay, stating that there was a passenger who had failed to board the aircraft after checking his bag and obtaining a boarding pass. For security reasons, the aircraft would not be allowed to take off with his luggage on board. I then breathed a belated sigh of relief now knowing that my little suitcase had never been involved.

After all the luggage was reloaded, we taxied to the runway and took off with an eastward heading toward Osaka. As we reached cruising altitude, the drink carts emerged, and I finally managed to relax. We were served dinner and offered a final round of drinks before the large overhead lighting domes were dimmed for the night.

I turned on my reading light and perused the headlines of the *International Herald Tribune.* Just as I had suspected, the headlines announced the arrival of the Ayatollah Khomeini in Tehran. He had arrived there yesterday morning at 9:30 on an Air France 747 from Paris. Our speculations at the Mehrabad International Airport concerning who was onboard the inbound 747 jumbo had proven to be true.

As I read further, I could see that the cleansing process had already begun. Tehran had a small red-light district with a handful of working prostitutes. The most infamous of all was Patteh Balonda (Tall Patteh), who was said to be more than six feet tall. I knew of her because the drivers at work sometimes jokingly teased me by offering to take me on a side trip to see Patteh. The revolutionaries had lined all the prostitutes up against a wall where they were executed by firing squad.

The newspaper article also included a story concerning several Iranian air force generals who were arrested and summarily executed. I read further and saw that my friend and working counterpart, General Ghorbani, was on the list. I could only imagine what he must have endured, and I didn't have a desire to read further.

I now fully understood why the Iranian air force had fled our office building. I then worried about Shapour and wondered about the fate of the four-star army general whose name I did not know. I had mixed feelings of anger as I stared out the window into the night and silently grieved for all the good people of Iran, including Freda, General Ghorbani, and even Patteh Balonda.

I was now more than a little amazed that I had managed to successfully move my bag of money out of Iran and through Greece and Turkey. My trip was downhill from there, as I faced only a brief refueling stop in Osaka and the American customs in Honolulu.

But I trusted the Americans and was confident that they would do the right thing. I had already decided that if they confiscated the money and later returned it to my company, that would be agreeable with me. I was just too exhausted about the whole thing to worry about it any more.

Thanks to the efficiency of the Japanese, the refueling stop in Osaka had gone smoothly and seemed like nothing more than a slight bump in the road. We were quickly on our way to Honolulu. After a sleepless night, I tried one more time to grab at least a fitful nap. As my mind began to wander, I thought about my home, my family, and an incident that occurred to me when I was only a child.

On one cool East Texas night, I could feel the chills as they started at the nape of my neck, quickly spread across my shoulders, and raced down along my spine to my legs where I could feel the hair standing on end with fear. For the first time in my twelve short years, I could clearly hear my heart pounding with alarm as I first noticed him in the shadows of our backyard. In the dim refinery light, I could barely make out that he was a big man, a stout man with a broad frame who stood at least six-five or six-six.

I could feel my muscles tensing, almost cramping with the dread of looming danger as I thought to myself, *Who is this intruder and why is he prowling here in our backyard? Is he here to harm me, my sister, Mother, or Daddy? Is he here to rob us or, even worse, to kill us? Maybe this is the same criminal who savagely attacked and robbed the Toppings. I just don't know.*

Our daddy was employed at the Hanlon-Buchanan Plant, which was a gasoline refinery near Gladewater in the East Texas Oil Field. This plant employed large, noisy vacuum pumps to pull the wet natural gas from the wellheads and then used an oil absorption method to refine the gasoline from the gas.

Hanlon-Buchanan Plant near Gladewater, Texas, in the East Texas Oil Field—the largest gasoline plant in the world's largest oil field

Daddy had the job title of operator. The operator's job was a responsible position and involved keeping the gasoline refining in operation around-the-clock. Shift work was required.

There were three shifts at the plant—the day shift, the evening shift, and the graveyard shift. Each shift was rotated once a week, so Daddy's sleeping habits changed weekly with his shift change. He was a dedicated, hard worker, and his undisturbed sleep was very valuable to him.

My older sister and I were conditioned at an early age to walk softly and to never raise our voices while he was asleep. The punishment for waking him was swift and sure, so we always tried to quietly be on our best behavior, making certain we never awakened him.

I always quietly stayed up late studying, doing my homework, and watching late-night television in the corner of our small living room. I was there on that night I have never forgotten.

It was a Sunday night at ten o'clock, and I had just finished watching *Gunsmoke*, which was my favorite Western television series. I could hear that pesky mockingbird just getting warmed up in his crepe myrtle bush on the south side of the house. He was early tonight, as he usually got started with his springtime song about midnight. Daddy used to threaten to shoot this bird because it sometimes disturbed his sleep, but I was relieved when he decided against it. Everybody knows you could have heaps of bad luck if you killed a mockingbird.

I was just putting away my books when I remembered my denim jeans and began mumbling to myself. "Damn, my blue jeans are wet."

I had two good pair of school jeans, which Mother would normally wash and hang out to dry on Saturday so they would be ready in time for school Monday morning. But she had washed them that day, and they would never be dry in time for school in the cool, humid night air. I would have to go out to the clothesline and bring them in to dry by the gas space heater in the opposite corner of the living room.

I opened the front door, stepped onto the porch, and turned left into the night air. It was cloudy with a slight breeze that evening, but there was always a dim glow from the nearby refinery lights that were on all night. I took another left at the corner of the house and proceeded toward the clothesline in the backyard. As I neared the clothesline, I could barely make out my jeans hanging near the middle. But when I glanced to the right, I saw him standing there.

A large, menacing man was lurking in the shadows of our backyard. It was then I suddenly realized that the intruder was in all probability the same one who had attacked and robbed the Toppings. As my heart began to pound, I immediately stopped in my tracks, turned around, and ran for the front door as if my life depended on it.

The Toppings were an elderly couple who lived alone on the isolated oil lease just to the east of us. They occupied a small, white wooden house provided by the lease. Mr. Topping was responsible for the day-to-day maintenance and operation of all the oil wells on the property.

By the winding road, they lived maybe a half mile away, but as the crow flies, it was not more than a couple of hundred yards. We were their nearest neighbor but could not see their house, as it was hidden away in the dense East Texas piney woods.

One night they were savagely beaten, robbed, and left for dead. They survived but never returned to their little white house in the woods, and it had remained vacant for several months. Their assailant had not been apprehended, and they described him as being a very large man.

I carefully opened the front door, entered the living room, and closed the door as always, taking care not to make too much noise. I silently tiptoed through the kitchen to the back bedroom where Daddy was sleeping. I then grasped the steel doorknob with the sudden realization I could not turn it. But it wasn't locked, nor was it broken. I just could not bring myself to open that bedroom door and wake Daddy for any reason. I knew then I would have to handle the matter myself.

I went to the living room corner near the space heater where three unloaded hunting guns were leaning in the corner. I would have my choice of weapons. There was a 12-gauge automatic shotgun, a 16-gauge pump shotgun, and a 22-gauge single-shot rifle. I knew the shotguns would be the most effective, but to load either would be entirely too noisy. I chose the rifle and quietly loaded it with one 22-gauge long rifle shell. I knew I was a good shot, and one bullet should handle the job.

As I stepped outside onto the front porch, I fumbled with the safety lever, as I could not remember if it was in the off position. Once assured the safety was off, I left the porch and again turned left at the corner of the house and quietly crept toward the backyard. I could just make out the form of the intruder near the right end of the clothesline.

I could now feel those fear-inspired chills race down my spine as I stood up straight, aimed the rifle at him, and in my most assertive voice demanded, *"Put your hands up and do not move!"*

He did neither. He did not put his hands up, and I saw him move slightly in my direction.

I then summoned all my courage, closed my eyes, and squeezed the trigger. I heard the sharp pop of the rifle, felt the slight recoil, and was immediately distressed when I opened my eyes and found him still to be standing. I understood that my one shot had missed, and I knew I was in more trouble than I could handle.

But I then realized something seemed wrong. I had just fired a shot at this man, and he should have either fled or attacked me by now. Something was just not right as I slowly inched forward to where I could see the intruder more clearly. He finally came into focus, and I could now see the intruder was not an intruder at all but a pair of Daddy's coveralls hanging on the clothesline to dry.

I now roused from my restless sleep as I heard the chime indicating that the smoking sign had been turned off. The familiar vibration was soon felt as the flaps were extended and the landing gear was lowered. The aircraft was now on its final approach to the Honolulu International Airport.

The stewardesses had already passed out the US Customs Declaration Form to each passenger. I had completed the form with the exception of the dreaded item Item 13. I couldn't help but feel a bit uneasy as customs had identified this particular item with such a wretched number. I wondered how I could get rid of this thirteenth since going on a picnic was not an option.

Item 13 stated: "I am (we are) carrying currency or monetary instruments over $10,000 or foreign equivalent."

There were two boxes that followed to be checked either yes or no. But because I knew I had to declare the money, I checked the yes box, convinced it was the only correct thing to do.

We then landed, taxied to the gate, and deplaned into the US customs terminal. I picked up my suitcase at the luggage carrousel and carried it to the line that formed at the passport checkpoint.

When it came my turn, the customs officer asked no questions but merely did a visual confirmation of my picture in my passport. He then stamped my passport with an entry stamp and welcomed me home. I proceeded to the inspection area and entered another line.

The inspection line slowly dwindled until it finally became my turn. I handed my passport and declarations form to the customs officer. She checked my passport and saw I had replied yes to Item 13 on the declaration form and asked, "Mr. Tipton, Are you bringing in currency or some other monetary instrument?"

I answered, "Yes, I'm bringing in currency."

She then asked, "What currency are you bringing in, and what is its total value?"

I replied, "I'm bringing in Iranian riyals worth approximately $253,000."

The customs officer was visibly impressed with the amount and unzipped my overstuffed suitcase for inspection, allowing several bundles of riyals to spill out in plain view. I then heard a hushed murmur rise from my fellow passengers in line behind me as they all saw the contents of my suitcase. The officer then filled out a form, handed it to me, and directed me toward secondary inspection for a further in depth interview and inspection.

There was no one waiting in line at secondary inspection, and I soon found myself being interviewed by another customs officer inside a private, partitioned room. The officer opened my suitcase and asked me where I had gotten the riyals. I explained to him that it was my company's money, and I was returning it to Fort Worth from the revolution in Iran. I then showed him my copy of the bank's check along with the account closure documents. He also confirmed my company identification along with my Iranian entry/exit visas that were stamped in my passport. We then counted the money, and the amount agreed with the total on the check and the account documents.

Everything appeared to be in order, and the customs officer seemed to be satisfied I had legitimately entered the country with the money. But I just couldn't believe my ears when he finally said, "Mr. Tipton, you are free to go."

I then mentally let out a big sigh of relief as my money burden had finally been lifted from my shoulders!

A wave of exuberant euphoria then swept through my body as I thought to myself, *I'm free to go, and the money is now mine! I'll just waltz outside to the nearby taxi stand and have the first limo driver take me to the best five-star hotel in all of Waikiki Beach. On the way, we'll stop at the first burger joint, and I'll order a double cheeseburger with real mayo and large fries with heaps of the ketchup that doesn't run. Then tomorrow I'll rent a car. Not just any car, but a brand-new, fire-engine-red 1979 Corvette convertible. Then I'll cruise around this little island in the style I now deserve. And when I get back home to Texas—*

If I had a fatal flaw, it had to be I could never resist being seduced by temptation. I was tempted by my ex-wife's striking beauty, although we had little in common. I romanced her, I married her, and I lost interest in her. She recognized this and divorced me. I was tempted to buy my jeep in Tehran and had to have it although another vehicle would have served me far better. I had now been tempted by the money and had felt like a drunken sailor out on the town ever since I decided to steal it.

It had been an exciting high-stakes game. But the game was now over, and I had won. It was now time to ease my conscience and return the money to its rightful owner.

I spent the entire week on the beach at Waikiki decompressing from my great adventure before returning to Fort Worth. Upon my arrival, I called Ray Cole and set up an appointment for the next morning at nine.

I arrived at Ray's office promptly as scheduled carrying my suitcase. I knocked on his door and stuck my head inside as always. "Hey, Ray, good morning! Got a minute?" I asked.

He laughed and got up from his desk to shake my hand. It was good to see Ray again, as he was now like an old friend. I set the suitcase unopened and lying on its side in the middle of his desk.

He was clearly surprised as he asked, "What's this, a present for me from the Ayatollah?"

I laughed and replied, "You'll see. Open your present!"

Ray then unzipped the suitcase and opened it, allowing the bundles of one-hundred-riyal notes to spill across his desk. He was totally taken by surprise, and I quickly gave him a brief explanation of how I had managed to rescue the money.

Word of the riyals on Ray's desk soon began to circulate in the office, and everyone wanted to take a look. Soon, a photographer from the *Shell Helicopter News* showed up and took pictures of Ray and me shaking hands and congratulating each other from behind the stack of money. The photographer assured us this picture would appear on the front page of the very next issue.

I knew then my long-held fantasy would now come true. Every managerial employee, including even the company president and CEO, would soon know my name. I was truly humbled knowing Shell would now take care of me as one of their own. At that moment, I felt I had finally achieved the job security I always longed for. I realized I would proudly be spending the rest of my working career with that little helicopter company in Fort Worth, Texas.

"Oh yeah," Ray said, "before I forget about it, Ben called from Tehran a couple of times trying to get in touch with you. He said he needs to talk to you about a job opening at the embassy."

Ray handed me a slip of paper with Ben's name and an unfamiliar Tehran telephone number scribbled across it.

He laughed and jokingly advised, "Give him a call. You never know!"

I suddenly felt the overwhelming allure of enticement and knew I had no choice but to succumb to my latest temptation. I couldn't wait to talk to Ben!

Epilogue

"Son of a bitch, Ben, what was that?" I asked.

We had both winced as we heard the nearby loud, metallic sound of metal crashing into metal at the US embassy's front gate in Tehran.

With a clear expression of concern etched on his face, Ben answered in his best Texas twang, "Yeah, I heard it, John-Boy. Never you mind the mules, just keep loading the wagon. You understand the importance of our mission. Just keep shredding!"

I replied with a hint of sarcasm. "Yes sir, Colonel! I'll just continue to calmly sit right here and shred this mountain of paper while the militant Iranian students are attacking our main gate!"

I disobeyed his order as I dropped my handful of documents and ran over to the nearby second-story window. I wanted to see if I could better determine what was happening outside our perimeter wall on Takht-e-Jamshid Avenue in front of the embassy.

It was November 4, 1979, and the government-backed Iranian students were continuing their hostile demonstrations just outside the American embassy wall. They were outraged that the US government had issued the dying Shah visa authorization to visit New York City for cancer treatment. They demanded instead that the Shah be returned to Iran to stand trial.

Telex instructions were earlier received from the State Department giving top priority to shredding every sensitive document in the embassy. Ben, as manager of administration, was put in charge of this operation.

We then heard the loud metallic crash again. I now watched as our battered front gate suddenly swung wide open, enabling the angry student mob to surge into the embassy compound!

In stunned disbelief, I shook my head as I pensively thought to myself, *My wayward Iranian brothers, che shodeh, che shodeh?*

The End

CPSIA information can be obtained at www.ICGtesting.com
Printed in the USA
LVOW06s0727160114

369582LV00001B/42/P

9 781491 706893